WITCHES OF MERCHANT CITY

Luke Belcourt

Publishing History

First cover: October 2021
Second cover: 2025

For more, visit lukebelcourt.com!

To Mum

This one would've fit right in

with your tartan doilies

author's notes

This is a book about being Glaswegian, and being a witch, and being a Glaswegian witch.

By definition, in writing it I tried to lift a smidge of the self-editing you do when you have a non-standard dialect and you're trying to sell stories to Americans and the English.

I've tried to avoid the use of footnotes and the like. I'm sure even the most... Caledonially challenged of yous are clever enough to follow along.

Thank you for reading!

chapter 1

Holly was already dreading going to work tomorrow with the hangover approaching like a storm front.

The night air was crisp and cold and clear, and she was sobering up quickly as she and Arabella staggered down Argyle Street towards home.

They didn't normally drink that much. They'd reached the age where they no longer got the bohemian rush of spending an entire night on the top floor of Polo, huddled in a group, breathing plumes of cigarette smoke out into the night sky like some sleeping dragon, or a factory chimney. She rattled in her pockets looking for bus fare, knowing her account was probably in the red and she wasn't getting paid until tomorrow.

Arabella stopped outside the McDonalds on the crossroads at Union Street, smiling, leaning on a transformer box. She looked that bleary-eyed, blissed-out way when you'd left the party at just the right time. With her back-combed hair, her frayed skirts and her willowy legs, she always looked like she was posing for an album cover.

"You wanting food?" Holly asked.

"Nah."

"Why'd you stop then?"

Arabella shrugged. "Just soaking it in." She looked up and down Union Street, and back along Argyle Street the way they had come. "You know Argyle Street has a typo in it?"

"What are you on about?"

"It's supposed to be two L's, no E. It's a surname. The longest artery in the city centre, and it's had a typo so long that it's just its name now."

"Why do you care so much about this stuff?" Holly laughed.

"Cos we walk down it every day!" Arabella scoffed. "Thousands of people do. Charging it up."

Holly rolled her eyes. "Could you take a holiday from the ley lines shite for *one* day?"

Arabella raised a hand in resignation. "Fine." With a Herculean effort she righted herself and looked the way they were going to walk. "But look!" she said. "They split the street in half! Jammed a motorway down the middle. And then, for thirty years, they left a bridge, hanging over the bypass that *goes nowhere*."

"I blame Thatcher," Holly said.

Arabella laughed. "I swear to God," she said. "When the Apocalypse finally comes, the portal to hell will open right there. Like a fault line in an earthquake."

Holly checked the clock on her phone lockscreen. "It's running a wee bit late, the Apocalypse."

Arabella sighed, like she always did when she knew she wasn't getting through. Holly beamed at her. It was the foundation that their friendship had always rested on — Arabella was all fairies and ley lines and chakras, and Holly was steel-capped boots, a mullet, and 'don't fuck with me'.

"Come on, Samantha Stephens," Holly said, taking her by the arm. "I've got work in —" she checked her phone again, "— five hours, Jesus…"

"I've got a lie in," Arabella said, smugly. "Call in sick!"

"I can't, I'm already on thin—" Something collided with her back with a crash.

Knocked from her feet, she hit the ground hands-first — the cold, wet kiss of the concrete on her palms, at once making them numb, tingling, prickling. Getting to her feet again, she smarted, wringing her hands to try and bring back the feeling. She looked at the back of her legs, the other source of pain. A large tyre track of mud ran up her calf.

Through the anaesthetic of booze, it only stung lightly but she turned to see what had happened. The transformer box Arabella had been leaning on now had a huge dent in it, and a mangled bike. The cyclist was staggering about. Full lycra gear, a skinny guy probably about ten years older than them. His hair was thinning under the cycling helmet. She could smell the booze off him from here, oaky expensive whisky.

"You okay?" she said to Arabella first, who was rubbing her lower back.

Arabella nodded, wincing, then turned to the cyclist. "You okay mate?"

The cyclist was looking at his warped bike, rubbing a knee which now had blood pouring down it. "You knackered my bike!"

"Mate, you drove right into the back of us!" Holly said.

"You're paying for a new one!" he said, tumbling towards them.

Holly got right up in his face. "You need to look where you're going!" His breath was heaving with the drink. He was drunker than they were, clearly too drunk to be cycling about at any rate.

He lunged with a right hook and clocked her in the side of the face.

The world spinning, her anger bubbled up and she rushed for him.

"Holly, stop! Let's just get out of here!" Arabella shouted, trying to hold her back.

"No, he's just cracked me!" Holly said. She turned to him. "Fuck you!"

The guy raised his fist again but stopped suddenly, hand suspended in mid-air. Frozen to the spot. He couldn't move an inch.

Arabella let go of Holly with her free hand, and Holly turned.

Arabella had her other hand raised, index finger clenched in thumb, as if she was holding an invisible marionette string.

"Are you...?"

"Let's just go," Arabella said. She looked like she was straining to concentrate. "Okay?"

"How are you doing that?" Holly said. But through the boozy haze, she had a weird feeling she already knew... Déjà vu was hitting her so hard she was starting to feel queasy. Like motion sickness.

"I'll explain later, we have to leave before—" Her hand snapped open as though the string was pulled, and he wrestled free. He grappled Holly and the two of them struggled for a moment before Arabella pulled Holly away again.

"Get back here!" he shouted. He grabbed the bike and with a clumsy gesture, lifted and lobbed it at them. Holly, who was still between Arabella and the guy, flinched.

But the bike stopped in mid-air. Holly blinked, confused.

She looked back at Arabella. Holly had never seen her look so furious.

The bike clattered to the ground. He stood, stupefied at the display.

Then Arabella crossed the distance between them and broke his nose with her forehead.

Holly whooped. "Oh my God, where did you learn how to do *that*?"

He was staggering, dazed, maybe concussed.

"Well, when a witch does it, we call it the Glasgow *Curse*," Arabella said. She looked... shock white, Holly thought. Shivering and pale as she clutched at the pendant round her neck, as if grappling with what she'd done.

He dabbed at his nose, no doubt expecting to see blood, but instead... roots had begun to sprout from his nostrils.

Little white tubers to start, but then quickly thickening, and multiplying. Wriggling green gorse climbing out, moss growing around his nostrils. He groaned, falling backwards, and by the time he hit the ground, a full tree had begun to sprout out of his head. It warped his skull as it forced its way out, the roots pushing through the concrete like fingers into the soil underneath.

Holly was speechless.

"Dear Green Place," Arabella said. She rubbed her head, hissing through her teeth like she had a headache coming on.

Holly could feel all the blood draining from her body. "How did you do that?"

"Let's just go before anyone finds us," Arabella said, grabbing Holly's hand. She was clammy, and cold. Terrified. "Come on, he'll be gone by morning, the city will absorb his nutrients."

But Holly was transfixed.

The tree had embedded itself in the building, growing into the foundations. It was starting to bloom now, gentle green leaves. The man's body jutted out from the base by his neck.

"Arabella," Holly said, holding both her friend's arms. "*How*, did you do that?"

"Well, Glasgow *is* a city which prides itself on being made out of people," she gulped. "People, it turns out, make very good compost."

Holly stepped back, looking up and down the pavement, the walls. She was suddenly aware of all the other plants growing out of the buildings on the street. In the city. Glasgow was full of them. Old Victorian buildings with trees bursting out of their foundations, out of the walls, branches spilling out into the street. Houses, reclaimed by nature, with people *still living in them*. Like squirrels in an old oak.

"This is... I don't..." Holly said.

"And I'm sorry, Holly," Arabella said.

Holly's headache was getting even worse now, her brain pounding like a steel drum, her mouth starting to salivate, she was about to boke.

"But I'm afraid I can't let you remember this."

Holly turned back to her friend just in time to see her wave her hand through the air, and the next thing she knew she was waking up in bed with a hangover.

chapter 2

The world was spinning. Lights went past quickly, in rhythm. Like a car speeding past streetlights. Holly was running. Arabella's hand was clammy in hers, both of them sweating and panting in fear as they ran. If they stopped, they died.

Now Arabella was standing by a door, investigating around the door jamb like she was looking for a gap.

"Are you sure this is the one?" Holly was saying.

"I think so," Arabella was saying. "There's a silence in it."

And then they were sitting on a train, the faded blue quilted fabric, the burning yellow-green light of the fluorescents overhead. Arabella had tear stains down her face, sobbing. Poor thing, Holly was thinking. In all their years as friends, she'd never seen her so distraught.

Arabella fought her panicking chest into deep breaths, wiping her tears away. "They're gonna kill her," she was saying. "They're gonna kill her and there's fuck-all I can do."

"I know," Holly was saying, and there was a certainty in her heart. In the distance, sirens. "I know. But don't worry," she continued, as the sirens grew louder, and louder. "I have a plan."

And then she realised the sirens were her alarm clock.

Her eyes flicked open. Her room was dark, and still the bombsite she'd left it when she'd fallen asleep, a mere handful of hours ago.

She sat bolt upright, pushing the covers back, her heart still jackhammering in her chest, though she struggled to recall what she'd been dreaming about. She reached for her phone to kill the alarm, and flicked the light on her bedside table, trying to work out the more transient question — was she still drunk or just hungover?

Flipping her legs over and putting her feet on the cold floorboards of the dingy wee flat, she pushed herself up before her body convinced her to go back to bed. She stepped to her dresser — not too clumsily, she thought. Probably just hungover. That was good. She didn't think she could take another sickie and get away with it.

She pulled a fresh pair of jeans and a t-shirt out of the dresser and had a wee peek through the blinds. Finnieston, in the pitch black, just as she'd left it. The streetlights on the main road cast a faint glow onto the wee shuttered shops across the street from them. She'd get a quick shower, and hopefully catch a coffee or something from the coffee shops that opened even earlier than *her* work did.

Padding through the house towards the bathroom, she passed Arabella's room, the door ajar. Arabella lay with her face down on her bed in her glad rags like she'd conked out on the walk home and landed on her bed by autopilot.

Holly shut Arabella's door, so the noise of the shower wouldn't wake her up and steeled herself for a truly dog-shite day ahead.

***

Holly leaned her head on the counter, the pressure squeezing some of the headache out like wringing water out a tea towel. The shop, nestled on the main thoroughfare of Buchanan Street, was normally dingy as a cave but every individual sunbeam making its way through the window was searing her eyeballs.

She groaned loudly, lifting her head and leaning back in the high chair that didn't let you relax while you were sitting. The flashing green LEDs of the cash register, the red of the CCTV, blinked like lasers at her.

"Well, I did tell you not to go out," Joann said. She was arranging the new window display, a tawdry tartan tablecloth arranged with postcards showing the Cairngorms and Loch Lomond, and an array of Highland Coos wearing kilts and Jimmy hats.

"D'you ever feel a bit like we're pimping out our culture working in here?" Holly asked.

Joann was barely listening. "You've clearly not worked in retail very long." She adjusted one of the larger Highland Coo's kilt, as though his willy was hanging out, and placed a large silver pocket watch in front of it. The pocket watches had nothing to do with Scotland, but they sold well, and they were very expensive. "It's all just shite," she said, dusting her hands. "Whether you're selling books, food, fridges or... whatever this crap is." She stood, brushing down the tartan skirt they were both forced to wear.

Holly had had four jobs and four managers in the last eighteen months, and Joann was probably the soundest. A less sound manager probably wouldn't have let her turn off the bagpipe cover of *We Are The Champions* that had played on loop for the last hour.

The jingling bell above the door rang in a sound that invaded Holly's dreams nightly, as the door opened. A large man in a cream polo shirt and a pair of khaki cargo shorts came in. He was wearing thick woollen Edinburgh Mill socks that looked brand new under his sandals.

Joann, still working on the window display, nodded insistently to

Holly, who put on the biggest fakest grin she could manage, and approached him.

"Hello sir, can I help you?" she asked, using her tourist voice to be more easily understood.

Bloody hell, he was a big guy. Holly wasn't short herself, not by society's standards anyway, but he was a good two heads taller than her, blocking most of the doorway as he came in. He had that look about him, like twenty years ago he'd probably been jacked through the roof, but now his skin had thinned a bit and the beer had reached his belly.

"Hey," he said. American. Unsurprising. Or maybe Canadian — she was only now starting to tell the difference. "I'm looking for a jacket pin."

"Of course, sir!" she said, ignoring the hangover making her head spin. "If you'd like to come over, we have a large num—"

"Yeah, it's O'Leary. I'm from the Scottish O'Learys," he said as he saw the brooch rack she was referencing — most of them were a variety of surnames.

"Ah, well unfortunately that's specifically an Irish surname so I don't know if we'll have one with that name," she said.

"No, it's Scottish. My great-grandfather came from Scotland."

Holly's temple twinged. "I'm sure he did, sir," she said. "But we won't have that name. We do have a number of ones that don't have a name o—"

"What about this one?" he picked up one that said *Reilly* on it.

"I mean..." She counted to ten inside her head. "That's a different name."

"I'll take it," he said.

Holly's eyes were about to burst. "I'm sure you will," she said, strained.

"What's that s'posed to mean?" he furrowed his brow, as though it was just now crossing his mind that she was annoyed at him. He pushed his shoulders back and looked down at her, all machismo.

Holly opened her mouth, but by this point Joann had arrived to rescue the man and make the sale.

"I'll take that over here thanks," she said, guiding him away. "Have you seen our scarves? They're lovely for the lady in your life."

He still looked annoyed at Holly, but seemed to think it wasn't worth biting, and allowed himself to be led to the register.

He thumbed the scarf. "Real tartan?" he asked.

"One hundred per cent Scottish wool," she said with a smile. The rehearsed half-truth was easier than explaining that a tartan scarf would be a bit thick and heavy, and even then, you wouldn't be selling it for a tenner. They both said this line multiple times a day.

"I'll take two," he put them on top of the Reilly brooch and started looking at postcards as Joann rung them up.

Putting his purchases in a wee bag that looked like a shortbread tin, she passed them over with a smile. "Thanks very much, enjoy your stay!"

"Thanks," he said, taking it and pushing past Holly to get out of the cramped little shop. Holly made no attempt to move for him. "By the way," he said, as he opened the door, and that infernal little jingle rang again. "I really am Scotch."

It was clearly meant to be some kind of argument win before slamming the door on them, but Holly exploded.

"*Scotch* isn't a nationality!" she shouted. "It's a drink!" Then her top blew. "It's not even a drink! It's not a real word! It's been called whisky for centuries, then you name your sugar water after it, and you make us change the name like a bunch of bloody hipsters!"

It kind of looked like he'd lost what she was saying through the Accent Fog. Joann, however, was white as a sheet.

"Holly," she said. "Back room. Now." She was shaking with rage.

Holly screamed through her teeth, then stormed into the back room.

***

Holly swirled the ibuprofen in her mouth as she tried to get her sandpaper throat to swallow them without any water in the back room.

Joann entered, looking angrier than Holly was used to seeing her. "What, the *fuck*, was that all about?"

"I'm fuckin' sick of this!" Holly said. "Every day we have to listen to these numpties just talking complete pish!"

Joann screwed her face up. "Holly, you've only worked here a month and a half."

"Exactly!" Holly said. "I don't know how you do it!"

"Well, what kind of fucking experience of Glasgow do you think that guy is going to go home and tell his family about?"

Holly shuffled awkwardly. She was too hungover for this.

"Do you think he's going to go back to America and tell them all how Scotland is just a wonderful place to be? Just let him have his shitty story!"

"But it's not real!" Holly said, picking up a highland coo off a shelf. "This is a, it's a fucking fiction!"

"My parents probably have a few of those in their house. Is it not real for them?"

Holly groaned. "You know it's not the same thing."

"Who gives a shit?" Joann said.

"We are not their Disney World!" Holly said. "It's a caricature!"

Joann rolled her eyes. "Alright, William Wallace. I don't know why this is the *bonnie glen* you've decided to die on."

Holly fizzed.

Joann took a deep breath. "We've had this conversation four times. I cannot deal with you haranguing our customers, especially not when you're fuckin' turning up hungover!"

Holly sensed where the conversation was going. "Joann, I—"

"No. Get out of here. You're fired," she said. She waved a hand.

She did look regretful about it, Holly thought. Not that *that* made much of a difference. She was too hungover to argue though, so she grabbed her leather jacket and left without bothering to say bye.

chapter 3

Holly's commute was usually a twenty-minute walk to get into town, but on this crisp afternoon, a solid six hours early, it seemed to vanish immediately as her thoughts went round and round in circles. Rent. Job hunting. Hungover. Rent. Job hunting. Hungover. Rent. Job hunting. Hungover. And then she was rounding the little cafe on the corner, and she was home.

It was a pokey wee flat that was more expensive than it should've been with the mould. She enjoyed living in Finnieston — Arabella had had to talk her into it — but she wasn't sure she enjoyed it to the tune of over half her wages. She messed about getting her key out of her jacket pocket and let herself into the close.

The cold, Victorian splendour was reflected in none of the actual flats in the building, Holly was sure. A mahogany staircase swept past mosaic tile walls. It smelled vaguely of cigars. One of her neighbours probably, though she wasn't sure which one. Overcome suddenly with a wave of hangover lethargy she hadn't been expecting, she put her hand on the banister, and began to climb.

There were a handful of weans loitering on the steps on her floor, playing Top Trumps or whatever weans played these days. You'd think kids would be happier outside, but they always seemed drawn to these liminal spaces. They grabbed up their things as they saw her approaching, like they were preparing to leave for the bomb shelter, and rushed around up the stairs.

Holly paused on her doorstep, watching the corner.

Three wee heads poked round the banister, like a Hanna Barbera cartoon. Mouths hanging open, catching flies.

"Yous lookin' for something?" she asked.

"I like your hair," one of them said, a wee girl. Someone had put her hair in a hairband, and then into a tumble dryer from the looks of it.

Holly stuck her tongue out at them, and they giggled, before opening her door and heading inside, feeling marginally better than she had for the last few hours.

***

She took her shoes off and papped them in the corner, stomping through the house, creaking the wooden floorboards, and flopping down on the faded green couch melodramatically. She was still in her jacket, but she couldn't be bothered taking it off.

Arabella looked up from her laptop, peering over the cats-eye glasses she wore for reading. "That was quick."

"I got fired," she said into the pillow.

"Aw, Holly... Again?"

"Again."

"What did you do this time?"

"Shouted at another fanny."

Holly heard the creaky floorboards as Arabella approached, and then the soft rub of a friendly hand on her shoulder. She turned so her head wasn't in the pillow, looking up at Arabella.

"Ah well. Was it fun at least?" Arabella said. Holly scooted up a bit so Arabella could perch on the lip of the couch like an owl.

"No, it wasn't fun!" Holly said as she made space. "He just looked confused! Like waving a torch around in front of a baby."

"You never liked Joann anyway," Arabella shrugged.

"I didn't... not like her."

"Didn't you call her an 'entitled shitlord' three weeks ago?"

Holly snorted despite herself and rubbed her exhausted eyes.

"Yeah... But I liked not starving to death. I'm sick of bloody job hunting."

Arabella nodded, pensively. When she couldn't think of a way to help, she asked, "D'you want a beer?"

Holly sat up. "Ooh, ya dancer."

"Good, I'm gasping," Arabella said, taking advantage of the free space on the couch to spread out like a cat. "Get me one as well."

Holly groaned. "Oh, come on. I just got fired."

"Exactly, you've got nothing better to do," Arabella said. When the joke didn't land, she sighed. "I'm sorry. That wasn't funny." She lay a head on Holly's shoulder.

"It's fine. You're right, I did hate that job," Holly said, staring into space as Arabella drifted off to open the fridge.

"You'll find your purpose. I'm sure of it," Arabella said, as she returned with two Coronas, caps popped off with the mist rising up.

"Nae lime?" Holly looked up with puppy dog eyes.

Arabella raised a net holding two fusty limes, like a shrivelled bawbag. "Gone off," she said.

"Fair enough." Holly put her feet up on the coffee table, picked up the remote and put on the telly. "Come sit with me," she said.

Arabella lay her legs across Holly as she typed on her laptop.

"What are you working on?" Holly asked, flipping channels.

"Work thing," Arabella said.

"I thought your work had no computers. Thingy didn't agree with them?" The name was avoiding her. The person who ran the place.

"Nah, they don't. That's why I'm doing it here," Arabella said. Arabella worked at some New Age... Hippy... thing. She'd tried to explain it to Holly, but it always went in one ear and out the other.

Holly snapped out of it as she realised she was just channel surfing. She took another sip of Corona as she settled on a Judge Rinder rerun. "I don't think I've seen this one before."

Arabella flipped the laptop closed and put it down on the coffee table, rubbing under her glasses. "God, I should put a wash on. Here, if you're not working can you become my butler?"

"What's the pay like?"

Arabella picked up the lime bawbag. "I can give you two shitey limes."

"That could be the title of our sitcom," Holly said. "Budge a sec." She nudged Arabella's legs so she'd move them, and she could get up.

"Where are you going?"

"To put on a wash before you can," she said, and then bolted out the room.

Arabella made to rush, then waved a hand when she realised she couldn't be bothered.

Holly padded round her room, picking up the clothes she could find and chucking them into an already overflowing basket. She picked up the jeans she'd discarded by her bed the night before and went through the pockets.

There was a big dark mark down the back, like a tyre track.

"Weird..." she said. "Here, Bella!"

"Yes, angel!" Arabella called through from the couch.

"Just how much did we have to drink last night?"

"Dunno. Enough?" she asked. "I don't feel that bad."

"I feel like shit, and... where the hell did this come from?" she walked back into the doorway and showed the tyre track.

Arabella blinked at it. "Um... no idea. You go mountain biking at some point?"

Holly scratched her chin. "Not a clue." She shrugged and put the jeans on top before carting the basket into the kitchen to stick the washing machine on. "Here! You doing anything tomorrow? Are you seeing..." she snapped her fingers. Fuck, what was his name again?

"I was thinking about it," Arabella replied before Holly could pull the name out of her head.

She struggled to keep her eyes open when Arabella talked about her boyfriend. Arabella was the kind of girl that called herself a disaster bi, but for some reason chose to spend the last year with some loser with a pencil moustache, intergenerational wealth, and a podcast. Holly had taken to just calling him Podcast Boyfriend in her head, and because of that she could never remember his name.

It was weird as well; she was normally quite good with names... And faces for that matter, but even thinking about it now she couldn't summon an image in her head. And Arabella had been dating him for a *year*. Every time she thought about it, she thought, 'I need to make more of an effort', but then it happened again. Come to think of it, it had been a while since she'd actually *seen* him...

Arabella poked her head through the door. "You didn't respond."

"Sorry hen, I was off in my own world," Holly said. "What did you say?"

Arabella brandished the well-fingered menu from the Chinese. It was sunlight-bleached, the paper thin and peeling after surviving the seven-odd years since they'd both left school and moved in together. "My treat?"

"Ooh, you're too good to me, Bella. I'll get you back."

"Och wheesht, it's one pocket," Arabella said, getting her phone. She still called them up like a boomer and went to pick it up herself. 'They're warmer, and the apps take most of the fee', was always her excuse.

Holly smiled. She didn't have much in this world. No family, not many friends. No job, as of today. But Bella always had her back. Ever since they were wee kids, the two of them had been Thelma and Louise, back-to-back screaming at the world.

She sat down on the couch and picked up her frosty Corona. She clinked it with Arabella's and raised it to the telly. "And Judge Rinder. I'll always have you."

***

Holly woke up the next day and spent a solid hour counting the flecks of peeling paint on the ceiling of her room. She had a lot to do today but with no-one to tell her to do it she was having trouble getting up. Eventually, groaning the entire time like a plastic bag getting the air squeezed out of it, she rolled off the bed and shambled through to the bathroom to brush her teeth.

Arabella was sitting on the floor in the living room, huddled in front of the mirror doing her mascara. She'd started backcombing her hair recently.

"You goin' somewhere?" Holly asked.

"Yeah, I've got a date. Remember? I said last night."

The cogs turned in Holly's brain. She'd forgotten. Again. "Oh yeah, that's right. My bad. I'm just nipping in the shower, do you need in?"

Arabella shook her head. Then she turned and posed her face. Her cheekbones glimmered with a pale blue undertone. "What d'you think? Okay?"

Holly didn't really do makeup herself. She'd spent her teenage years dismissing it outright, even while Bella had waxed lyrical about it. It had always been her passion. With age, Holly had mellowed into 'you do you'.

"Stunnin', doll,", she said, and she wasn't lying. Even knowing nothing about it, she could appreciate it. It was a magic all its own, like needlepoint or antique restoration or any of those other things that she was only peripherally aware of but saw other people doing.

Arabella snorted. "You're a chancer," she said, turning her attention back to the mirror.

Holly did a little faux-curtsey, before moving through to the bathroom as she'd been intending.

The entire sink was surrounded on all sides by stuff. The detritus of two twenty-somethings holding siege on the bowl: paracetamol and tampons and Arabella's hormone kit and toothpaste and razors.

Rather than dealing with any of it, Holly picked it up in a big pile and moved it over to the side table by the shower. There was already another pile there, with a lot of the same things she had in her hands, but right now she only needed her toothbrush.

Setting a timer on her phone for three minutes to make sure she didn't skimp, she put her tunes on and stuffed the handset between the hand soap and the toothbrush holder, turning on the electric shower to give it time to heat up.

***

Holly emerged, having hair-sprayed her mohawk up just how she liked it. The ginger roots were starting to come through on the red, but it was at that stage where it looked intentional. She stood in front of the mirror above Arabella, standing at different angles. She didn't like wearing a tie, but needs must.

"Do you think this is professional enough?" She was still wearing her leather jacket over the shirt-and-tie combo, but it worked for Jake

Peralta. It made her look quite trim as well, gave her this pleasantly square silhouette.

"You going job-hunting?"

"I thought I'd pop in and ask Caesar for my old job back." His name was Cesar, but everyone called him Caesar.

"Pal, you look like a million quid," Arabella said.

Holly beamed. "Thank you." Then she squinted. "You going somewhere?"

"Yeah. I've got a date tonight. Remember?"

"Oh yeah," Holly said, shaking her head. She rubbed her chin. "Did you tell me about that like five minutes ago?"

"Yeah," Arabella said, and she looked a little sad. *Aw, fuck sake Holly,* she thought to herself. *Now I've hurt her feelings.*

"Sorry."

"What? No, don't worry about it!" Bella scoffed.

"Well, I hope you have fun at your..." It was gone again. What?

"Date," Bella finished.

"Yes. Date. ... What the fuck is wrong with me?"

"You've got a job interview in fifteen minutes?" Arabella said, like she was trying to get her out the door.

"Yes! Sorry! I'll be back! Don't wait up!" Holly saluted and went to put on her shoes.

"I'll hang a sock on the doorknob!" Arabella shouted jokingly after her.

Holly let the door close behind her, resolving to get Arabella one of her wee mystery novels or something to make it up to her. She didn't know what was up or down today. Hangover fuzzy-brain? But it had been happening so frequently...

chapter 4

Arabella eyed her handiwork in a compact mirror as she walked. She'd gotten ready too early, and like every time she did, all she could think about was the likelihood that when she popped out to the shops a bus would splash her Bridget Jones style, or a seagull would shite on her head, or the horizontal Scottish rain would destroy all her work. A dangerous thought pattern for any witch, since you might accidentally make it happen.

Throwing the mirror into the bottom of her bag, she sped up. She couldn't shake the weird cocktail of emotions in her stomach. She was so wired. Excited for tonight, she'd been waiting for ages. But she couldn't think about it for long because her mind kept flashing images of that guy, the roots bursting out his eyeballs, his death moan...

She'd never done that before. She'd seen other people do it. As spells went, it came easy to Glasgow witches. The magic equivalent of putting someone's finger in an electrical outlet. Plug them into the city, into nature.

She shivered, and realised she was walking so fast she was almost running.

She stopped. Took a breath. Centred herself. Tried to think clearly.

Had she gone too far this time? Was that the final straw?

There was a noise from her bag and she jumped, before realising it was her phone. She pulled it out of her pocket. Bloody contraption...

"BAWJAWS calling..."

Holly's contact picture stared at her, unchanged for a decade — a fuzzy old webcam photo of a stocky teenager with greasy hair, holding an HB pencil between her nose and her lips, eyes crossed for the camera.

She smirked, and picked up, the mere presence of her friend sending the stress pattering away like mice. "Awrite big man?" she said loudly into the phone.

"Oh good, you're actually carrying your phone for once," Holly said. "Listen, I'm just getting into town but I've just gone past that funky bookshop and there's folk in for—"

"The Yellow Tourmaline thing?"

"Aye, that's the one! Aw, did you already know about it?"

"Yeah, sorry. I pre-ordered it. Thanks for thinking of me though."

"That's what I'm for, babes," Holly said, making fake kissy sounds down the phone before hanging up on her.

Bella laughed, rubbing the bridge of her nose as she put her phone away.

Of course it was worth it. Holly was fine. And happy. And safe.

Right.

She was going to put the nastiness of last night behind her, move the guilt of The Situation to one side, and go get a bottle of wine for her date. Goddess knew it had been a while since they'd had some alone time without whispering to stop Holly hearing from the other room.

She was halfway down the street when she remembered she'd run out of chalk for the circle, and made a mental note to pop into Auntie's on the way home to get some of the good stuff off her.

The bell over the newsagent's door tinkled — Dal's was one of the few places that hadn't swapped out for one of those electronic beep-a-whosits. She had a peek down the aisles one-by-one, tentatively seeing if Dal was about. There was no-one on the till.

Scooting past the biscuits before she could be tempted by their golden luxurious wrappers, she eyed the fruit and veg in unassuming green baskets. She plucked a few of the healthier looking tomatoes and carrots. It couldn't compete with the factory-produced superfood from the supermarket, but she'd been coming in here since she was wee and she always felt better about shopping here.

A snotty kid came poking up the aisle, seventeen or thereabouts. She'd met him before — Dal had him working part-time. He said nothing, of course. His jaw clenched looking at her like he was trying to say something.

She smiled airily. "Good morning!"

He huffed and got back to work.

"Is Dal about?"

He looked at her, said nothing, and went back to what he was doing.

She clicked her tongue, making a big show of remembering. "Right. Of course."

"Is that wee Bella I'm hearing?" came a warm voice shouting from the back. It was followed by Dal himself, a portly, older Sikh guy whose age hadn't reached his eyes. He beamed from behind a big moustache and beard that was shock-grey. "Alright hen, how's it gawn? You've not been in for a few days, I was about to send out a search party."

Arabella grinned. "It's going okay. Work's been hectic." She'd been coming in here since she was a little kid. He'd used to let her climb under the milk cabinet and excavate the dusty change people had dropped, which she then immediately spent on sweeties and sticker packs, or on one very lucky day, a magazine. If there was one example that had shattered all her notions that transphobia was a product of age, it was Dalbir. "How've you been? How's Jas doing?"

"Och she's up to her neck with work, as usual. I phone her every few weeks to make sure she's remembered to eat," Dal said, picking up a cardboard box of onion rings and refilling the shelf. Jas was just older than Arabella, she'd moved down to London to do architecture or something. "I'm doing alright. Thinking about going down to see her for a bit, I need a bloody holiday."

"Well, tell her I was asking for her."

"I'll do just that," he put the box down and clapped his hands. "Right, what can I get you."

"Wee bottle of the house red, I think," Arabella smiled.

He approached the alcohol behind the counter like a sommelier. "Sounds good. I've got the Merlutt or the Cabernitt," he said, gesturing to the two rows of red bottles on the shelf. "Or the local vintage." He gestured to the row of Buckfast above them.

"Hmm..." she scratched her chin. "I think the Merlot. Splash out, why not."

"You going to a friend's house?"

"Nah, having one up."

"They're two for a tenner," he picked up the Merlot and waggled it like a tombola prize.

"How can I resist?" She reached into her handbag and got her purse out.

While she did, he looked over her shoulder. "Haw! John! Down the road and pick up the newspapers, would you?"

The disgruntled teen nodded and walked out.

"I would've chucked him by now. I'm doing his dad a favour, he's a bloody layabout. Tell you what, he quiets doon when you come in though. Can you stick about?"

She snorted. "Maybe I intimidate him."

"From the sounds of it, most women intimidate him. Some of the stuff he spouts. I swear, the internet was a mistake." He rang up the wine and took her money. "D'you need a carrier bag?"

"Do I need a carrier bag..." she scoffed. She pulled a canvas tote bag out of her handbag.

He rolled his eyes. "Aye, the turtles will thank you."

She smiled and slotted the stuff into her bag, being careful not to put the tomatoes somewhere they'd squish. "I'll see you about, Dal."

"Aye Bella, see you soon aye?"

And with that, she nodded out.

The kid, John, almost walked into her on the way out as he came in with the papers. He recoiled. Like she had a disease he worried was infectious. Despite everything, it still stung.

She smarmed. "What's the matter? Cat got your tongue?"

He gritted his jaw and he pushed past her back into the shop. She chuckled.

She'd been told growing up that if you didn't have anything nice to say, you shouldn't say anything at all. Clearly this kid had never gotten the memo. Eventually she'd had enough of him throwing abuse at her and she'd put a spell on him. Now, he wasn't allowed to open his mouth within a thirty-foot radius of a trans person. And he couldn't tell anyone why.

Honestly, she did wonder sometimes if she was an evil genius.

chapter 5

Holly made it all the way to the restaurant front. She was feeling pretty good, all things considered. Things were looking up, and Caesar had never been able to say no to her.

And then she'd seen Rachael through the front window. Working the bar.

Shit.

If Rachael was working there, she'd have no chance. Even if she got the job, it would be a living hell. Rachael was one of those bitter exes who would just never let it go. Holly had spent the last eighteen months swerving her at Del's whenever she saw her.

As if on autopilot, she drifted away from the window so she wouldn't be seen, and wandered down the street, finding herself outside a newsagent's at Trongate.

God, she could do with a cigarette. But they only came in twenties now anyway, and it was maybe not a good idea to light a tenner on fire for no reason, especially when she'd—

Wait, *had* she been smoking last night? It was unusual for her to black out memories like this. It created a deep, uneasy pit in her stomach.

"You look lost, hen," came a voice. "You okay?" It was a deep voice, but gentle and mellifluous. She looked up and realised she'd sleepwalked right through Trongate and was halfway to Glasgow Green.

The voice had come from a person standing under the bridge, smoking a rolly. They were tall — taller than Holly — with long blonde hair scooped into a messy bun. They wore a frilly shirt like a vampire, and a maxiskirt, and they grinned through wonky teeth and manicured facial stubble.

"Yeah, I'm good," she said. "Do I know you?" She was having déjà vu again.

The person raised a sculpted eyebrow. "I usually make a stronger first impression. Are you not Arabella's flatmate?"

"Yeah...?" Holly said. She wasn't surprised Arabella was the link — this person looked appropriately New Age.

"We met at the..." the person said, then trailed off. "Never mind." They were looking at her funny, like Sherlock Holmes examining a corpse. "I'm Roman. He/him pronouns." He put his hand out.

"Holly. She/her." She took his hand, and he shook it warmly with both of his, perching the rolly precariously on one lip to do so.

"How's she doing?"

"Arabella?" Holly said.

"Yeah," Roman said, smiling. Behind his eyes gears seemed to be turning. It was making Holly uncomfortable. However, she could smell the cigarette in his hands, and it was making her stomach dance.

"D'you mind if I tap one of those off you?" she pointed.

"Sure," he said, stubbing his dout on the bridge to roll another.

She looked up and down the street, the place was pretty much deserted other than them. "D'you live around here?"

He laughed. "You kidding? Do I look like I can afford a flat in Merchant City, hen?" He tapped the tobacco down with painted fingernails and licked the paper to seal it. "You really don't remember me at all, do you?"

"Sorry, no. Was it from last night? I blacked out."

"Nah, it was from a few weeks ago. I work with Arabella at the Archive." He pointed up the street with one hand as he held the cigarette out with the other.

She took it and looked where he was gesturing. The Merchant City Archive was nestled in a corner of the plaza across from the car park, in between an old record store and a vintage clothing shop. Nothing about it from the outside seemed to give away what its purpose was, the name painted along the top of the black storefront in silver calligraphy.

"D'you know I've never been in there," she said absently, taking a drag of the cigarette, which she hadn't realised until now was already lit.

"Yeah, that's... what you said last time," Roman said, his eyebrows furrowing. "Anyway!" He smiled. "I'm sure there's a reasonable explanation. I should be getting back to work."

"Sure. Well, it was lovely to meet you, Roman. Thanks for the cig."

"Good to see you, *again*," he said, a devilish twinkle in his eye, and he sauntered back up the plaza towards the Archive, his high heels clicking on the brick.

Holly stood there, finishing the cigarette. She was a hundred percent sure she'd never met him before, but she hardly thought he was lying.

She shrugged. Well, if Caesar's was fucked, she may as well head home.

***

Holly popped her key in the door. The flat was dark, with all the lights out, even in the middle of the day. "Hello?"

Arabella had made it sound like she was going to be in all afternoon… "Hello?" she asked again.

Every creaking floorboard seemed to scream as she tip-toed through the house.

She could hear whispering. Arabella and another voice from within her room. "Oh shit…" she said. Maybe she had that nightmare Podcast Boyfriend back. A thin sliver of candlelight peered out from under her cracked door.

The voice was far too deep for that though, she thought.

Sick of fumbling in the dark, she tried to flick the light on.

Nothing.

Fuse box must have blown again. Shit. The fuse box was in Bella's room.

She chapped the door, as quietly as she could. "Bella? Sorry…"

The door swung open by itself.

Arabella was sitting in the center of a circle drawn in chalk on her floor. Candles everywhere. There was a whoosh of air as if something had fled the room.

"Shit! What are you doing back?" her voice sounded weird, like she was talking from down a tunnel.

"Caesar was…" she said. "Wait, what the fuck is going on?"

"I—" The chalk circle underneath Arabella started to glow and disappear as though it were soaking through the floorboards. And then, she was gone. Like a black curtain had fallen over her, she vanished into thin air.

"Bella?" Holly said. From muscle memory, she flicked the light switch. For some reason though, it worked now. The room lit up.

But there was no-one here. She was gone.

"Arabella?" she said again, starting to panic.

She began turning the room upside down, as though she was going to find her under a pile of books.

Pulling out her phone, she opened Contacts and typed in 'Bella'.

The dial tone beeped three times as though it was trying to find a signal.

Then it spoke, with a clipped pan-loaf voice she'd heard a million times, though never on a phone line. *"This train is for: Glasgow Central Medium Level. This train will call at Anderston, Dalreoch, Coatbridge Sunnyside, Motherwell, Exhibition Centre, Gourock, the Seventh Circle of the Goblin King, Camelot, your mother's knitting cabinet, 12 BC, MySpace.com..."*

She looked at her phone as the woman continued to speak. "What the hell...?"

She tried WhatsApp.

A deep man's voice from the radio. *"... showers, thundery for a time. Good, occasionally moderate. Cromarty, South-West..."*

Facebook Messenger?

"The number you have dialled is a complex number, which can only be represented by a real number, multiplied by the imaginary unit 'i', which is defined as the square root of minus 1. Please hang up and try again earlier."

This didn't make any sense. It didn't add up. She'd been right in front of her, it was like —

She gasped as she remembered, dropping her phone as her hand went slack. She heard the crack of the screen as her mind raced.

Arabella had done this before.

Last night, she'd grown a tree out of a man's head, and she'd waved her hand and Holly had forgotten.

Weeks ago, she *had* met Roman! In the Archive!

And the podcast boyfriend! She'd never actually seen him! How did she know what he looked like?

He wasn't real.

Her head began to pulse, a migraine approaching like a storm coming in over the sea. She gripped her hands to her head, and she felt pathways in her brain that had been boarded over begin to open, light shining down them.

"What the fuck have you done?" she staggered to the kitchen, going through the drawers, vision blurring as the migraine hit like a freight train. Her stomach wrenched with queasiness, she needed to lie down, she needed to...

She clutched at the sink like a life raft, and vomited.

chapter 6

She lay in the dark on the couch, curtains drawn, all the lights off, head pounding for hours. But she couldn't stop her mind from racing, filling with memories that she'd somehow overlooked. She was desperate to get up, and get answers, but her whole body ached as the migraine washed over her.

So she sat, alone with only her thoughts, waiting for it to pass. If it would pass at all. It felt like it might just get worse until it killed her. The pain ached in her bones, her teeth.

Then her eyes opened. She'd fallen asleep.

She sat up. The pain had gone, mostly. She stood up, resting her feet on the floor. And she knew exactly where she had to go.

***

Holly banged on the door of the Archive. By now the sun had gone down, and the tiny neon LEDs which lit the plaza tried valiantly to hold back the blanket of night, but it meant nothing to the winter.

"Come on…" she said, banging again and again. The doors were shuttered, but she had a horrible feeling that if she went home and waited 'til morning the memories might fade again, or the migraine might come back. And they definitely kept odd hours so…

She banged again and again, calling, "Let me in! Are you in there?" until eventually, there was a rattle behind the shutters, and the sound of locks unpicking.

"Hang on, hang on!" came a voice she knew. Deep and gentle. Roman.

Eventually, the shutter came up, and she could see him. He was wearing a nightgown, with a fluffy purple dressing gown over it. "Holly?"

"Your name is Roman Buchanan, you've been a friend of Arabella's for many years," she said, trying to get the words out as fast as she could. "You like terrible music, good wine, and you've never remembered Arabella's birthday once." It was like saying it was a charm to stop her forgetting again. Arabella had talked about Roman all the time, of course she had.

A genuine smile spread across his face. "You *do* remember!"

"I think she made me forget somehow."

His face creased with concern. "Yeah, I thought that might be it. That doesn't sound like her."

"Why did she do that? *How* did she do that?"

Roman looked behind him and swallowed. "I suppose you should probably come in." And he stepped back and bid her enter.

***

She stepped past the door, foot scraping something, and looked down to see the shop had a trail of table salt across the door, which she'd tread on and broken.

"Sorry," she said, taking her jacket off as Roman poured more to fix it.

"No worries, I should've mentioned," he said. He checked his watch. "Bloody hell, it's late."

"What time is it?" she asked.

"Two." He rubbed his eyes. "Well, not going to get any sleep now. I may as well get the coffee on."

The room was open plan and large, like it had once been a restaurant of some kind. They were standing in a small foyer area that had a little set of steps leading up to a larger area that looked part-New Age shop, part-living room, and part-library. Roman crossed the stairs, heading towards one corner, where an espresso machine was sitting with sugar and coffee. Filling it with water from a little sink, he put it on a nearby hob and gestured for her to sit at the big wooden table that islanded the section of the room.

She did so, gingerly, not wanting to touch anything in case she broke it. The aesthetic of the room was of hyper-clutter and hyper-organisation, and everything looked like an antique.

Roman pulled a scrunchie from his pocket and hastily pulled his waist-length hair into a ponytail, little blonde curly flyaways still trying to escape capture. He sat down opposite her and put his hand out expectantly.

"What?"

"Your palm," he said.

"Oh, uh..." She felt a bit uncomfortable about offering it, but she did so anyway. She watched him turn her hand over in his delicate fingers, like a watchmaker inspecting an old timepiece, turning his head to look at odd bits.

She coughed eventually, breaking the silence. "Find anything interesting?"

"You're left-handed," he said. "That's pretty interesting."

"How did you work that out?"

"Because you gave me your left hand." The espresso machine started to whistle, and he got up to sort it. "Coffee?"

"Gasping for it," she said. "But did you find anything out about what happened to me?"

"What?" he said, confused. Then he realised the connection she had drawn. "Oh, no. I just need the practice. Do you take sugar?" He held up the espresso machine. She shook her head, and he poured it into two little espresso cups and brought them back to the table. "So, what do you want from us?"

"I need to find Arabella."

Roman's brow furrowed. "Did she go somewhere?"

"She vanished right in front of me!"

"Where to?"

Holly blinked. "Am I having a stroke or something? I don't know where!"

"I see," Roman said, sipping the espresso, taking a deep breath and closing his eyes. "Oh, sweet caffeine... Okay. I'm ready. Tell me everything."

***

"Oh, that's not good," Roman said, getting up from the table. Holly realised her coffee had gone forgotten during the story. She drank it in one go — freezing cold.

He was rattling through a drawer full of rolled-up papers, discarded lighters, and general detritus, before he came back with a large, old-looking map of Glasgow.

Grabbing the other cup off the table to unfurl the map over it, he pulled a necklace from under his nightgown and let it dangle loosely over the table. It circled above, as though along a magnetic field.

"It's not finding her…" he said, voice starting to crack with worry.

"What does that mean?"

"It means I need a bigger map," he said, pulling up the little chain and going back to the drawer. He pointed off down a side door. "I need you to go down the hall, second door on the right. Chap and tell the woman in there to wake up, it's an emergency."

"Right…" she said. She started to move, then stopped. "Just, so I'm on the same page as you."

"Yeah," he said, only half paying attention as he slammed the drawer shut and made for a bookcase off to the side.

"This is… *magic*, right?" she said. "You're all some kind of…"

He looked up. "Witches. Yeah."

Her stomach dropped. "Right."

"Remember," he said, making sure he made perfect eye contact. "You're always safe here. But your friend is a witch. One of our own. Thank you for bringing this to our attention."

"You're all witches," she said, still in shock.

He smiled, his crooked teeth beaming. "Welcome to the Coven of Merchant City."

chapter 7

The corridor was dark and lit only by halogen bulbs that were almost orange in their dimness. Shaking, Holly chapped the door.

"What is it, Roman?" came a voice from inside. Lilting, Hebridean. Older.

"Um, it's not Roman," she said. "He asked me to come get you; he says it's an emergency."

There was a ruffling from inside. The door opened a crack and a face peered out. A woman in her fifties with raven-black hair and skin so pale it was almost translucent. She looked Holly up and down, then said, "Five minutes." And she slammed the door shut in Holly's face.

Holly walked back to the main room, where Roman now had a large atlas of the world made from heavy-looking vellum paper rolled over the table. He was spinning the pendant above it again, but it was as indecisive as it had been before.

"This isn't good. Oh, this isn't good…" he was muttering to himself. "If the scry can't find her, it means she's either hiding herself, or she's left this plane entirely."

"There was a circle drawn in chalk on the floor," Holly said, trying to be helpful. "It disappeared with her though."

"What on earth could she have been doing? And why wouldn't she tell us about it?" Roman said. He looked up, and then looked around Holly. "Where's Iona? Did you not get her?"

"She said five minutes," Holly said, shifting from foot to foot. She felt like she was in the waiting room of a hospital.

"Think, Roman, think…" Roman said. "Where else can we rule out…? If she's in Elf-hame or one of the Nine Rings no scry is going to get through…"

"Sorry, Nine Rings?" Holly was starting to panic. "You think she might be in Hell?"

Roman shrugged. "No idea, hen. She could be fuckin' anywhere. Honestly, it was very rude of her not to leave a note. *IONA!*"

"*What?*" came a shout back.

"*Hurry the hell up!*"

"I'm coming, I'm coming!" Iona shouted back, irritably, walking through the door. She was fully dressed, hair in a braid and a long, elegant blue dress, the pyjamas of a minute ago vanished. "What's the matter, dear?" she said, watching him run around in his nightgown. Her eyes flitted from the maps on the desk to the pendant clutched in his hand. "Looking for someone?"

"Arabella's missing. Her flatmate saw her disappear in what sounds like a Sending Circle."

"Well then, scrying on her will be a waste of time," she said matter-of-factly. She turned to Holly, looking her up and down again. "I hope you don't have anywhere to be, young lady. We may be here a while."

"Uh, no. No, I don't," she said, as she realised she really didn't. All she had was Arabella. She tried to ignore the empty feeling that realisation put in her stomach. "How can I help?"

"I think our first port of call should be to find out exactly what our dear Bella was doing," Iona said. "With your permission, we'd like to reach into your memories."

***

The wooden floor was so cold it seeped through her jeans into her bones. She tried to fight her inner sceptic as Roman placed candles in a circle around them, and she sat across from Iona, who had her eyes closed and was breathing deliberately and rhythmically. In through the nose, out through the mouth.

"Budge up," Roman said to Holly, as he lit the last candle in the darkened room and pulled his nightgown up to keep it out of reach of the flame.

Holly scooted over, and Roman sat next to them, the three of them now forming an equilateral triangle. Roman closed his eyes and began to breathe in time with Iona, and Holly found herself joining in without really meaning to.

With the three of them now breathing in unison, Iona spoke.

"Our future unclear, our fellow witch hidden /
Let Holly's memories show unbidden."

A wind picked up. Holly opened her eyes, and the candles were flickering, barely staying lit. She felt her chest heave and her lungs filled with air—

She was standing in Arabella's room. Holly was watching herself standing on the phone. The whole image was shimmering, like a recreation made from raindrops bouncing off invisible objects.

"I remember this," she said. She could feel the inner sceptic inside her suffocating to death. This was beyond the pale. There was no rational explanation for any of this. It was real.

40

"I should hope so," Roman said. "We're pulling it out of your brain after all." He and Iona were in the room as well now, completely opaque against the flickering image of the dream space. They were looking around, taking in all the details, like detectives.

"But this is after she's already gone," Holly said.

Roman picked up a book from the desk and flipped it open. All the pages were blank. "I take it you never read any of these…"

Holly shot him a sarcastic look. "Her secret magical tomes? No."

He flipped it shut. "Dammit, even the titles are obscured." The text was out of focus, like a blurred photo.

"We have to go back further," Iona said. "Holly, hold your breath." She started spinning her hands like she was winding twine around her fingers, and the image started to reverse like a video tape.

Holly's phone flying up off the floor into her hand, Holly walking backwards out the bedroom door. The door closed and the image immediately disappeared, leaving them standing in blackness. Iona snapped her fingers, and the door opened, revealing some of the image again.

Arabella, terrified. Surrounded by candles. Not unlike them sitting on the cold floor of the shop as they spoke now. Holly could still feel the wood on her jeans, on her hands. They must still be sitting there on some level…

"Holly, focus please," Iona said, inspecting the tableau of Arabella being discovered. The whole image was starting to blur.

"Sorry," Holly said, trying to picture exactly what happened. Arabella herself started to come into focus, but the details of the chalk circle were smeared.

"It's definitely some type of Sending Circle," Roman said, pulling his dressing gown around him as he stooped to have a look at the other side of Iona.

"It's hard to tell how many rings she's drawn…" Iona said.

"I didn't get a good look. I think I maybe saw more when the light was *turned on."*

"You turned the light on?" Roman said, looking up. "Show us."

Holly looked at her own image in the door. "God, it's not exactly flattering to see yourself from this angle, is it?" She ignored the voice in her head pointing out everything she hated in the mirror, as she concentrated. Her image started to move, having their conversation in silence. The Image Holly's hand reached for the light-switch, and the detail of the room suddenly opened up.

"Okay, it looks like it's either four or five rings. Which means she was going somewhere very *far away," Roman said. "Can you remember any more?"*

Holly looked at it. "I don't think so?"

"Don't push it too hard," Iona said. "If you really don't remember, your brain will start making up details."

Roman looked at the still image of Arabella, looking up in shock at Holly in the door. "Why on earth have you done this, Bella..."

"Did you hear who she was talking to?" Iona said.

"It was... I thought it was that podcast-y boyfriend of hers."

"Boyfriend?" Roman looked confused. "She has a boyfriend?"

"I don't think he was real. I think she put him in my head when she took my memories."

"Why would she go to all this trouble though?" Roman said. "And why would she not tell us? You're her best friend, right? She must have a reason..."

"We have to find her," Iona said. "I think we've got all we're going to get. Holly?" she said, sounding not unlike a stern schoolmaster.

"Yes?"

"Put your hands up like this, if you please." She gestured raising her hands so her thumbs and index fingers formed a circle.

Holly copied her, and then Iona brought her hand down and broke the circle.

They all gasped as their eyes opened, back in the room. The candles had burned down, and the sun was starting to come up outside.

Iona got to her feet. "I'm going to consult my grimoire. I suggest you both get some sleep."

Roman turned to Holly. "You can sleep here if you like." Then his face dropped when he saw she was crying.

She wasn't even really aware she'd been doing it. She wiped the tracks from her cheeks. "Yeah, okay. Sure."

"Are you okay?"

Holly looked at the wet tears in her hand, cursing her traitorous eyes.

Roman clasped both his hands around hers. "Let's get a cup of tea and talk about it."

***

Other than the few hours she'd been unconscious with the migraine, Holly was now starting to feel the fact that she'd been awake for almost twenty-four hours. Her bones were starting to ache, and she was aware of a need to shower and change clothes. Still, she was too exhausted to do anything about it, so she sat at the kitchen table and let Roman bring her a cup of tea.

It was pretty good, she thought, even if he had put too much sugar in it.

"What's got you upset?" he said.

"You sound like Arabella," she said, smiling weakly into the cup, letting the steam warm her face. "I don't know, I guess I feel... a little violated? She was rooting around in my brain and I don't even know why?" She heard her voice crack as she said it and she tried very hard to tamp down her feelings.

"I'm sure there'll be a logical explanation. You know Arabella."

"Do I? It's starting to seem like a lot of it was lies."

Roman thought about it for a second. "I know, a lot of your details of her might be wrong. But you've known her a long time. And she does love you. I may have only seen the two of you together for a short time, but I could tell you had a strong bond. Hell, even I remembered you right?"

"Yeah..." Holly said. She gulped. "Honestly, the events of me being here for that night are still... fuzzy. What were we doing? It was like a book release or something?"

"Of sorts..." Roman laughed. "I'd just filled my first grimoire. It's... sort of like a witch life event."

"Right..." Holly said. "And I... didn't have any questions about that?"

"I mean, I did think it was a bit strange," Roman said. "But you seemed to know everything, and I didn't really have time to ask questions. It was kind of a big day for me." He cringed.

"Right..." Holly said. She tried to dig into her brain. Even the returned memories were fuzzy, like they'd been atrophying in her brain while she'd forgotten them.

"It's weird though," Roman said. "If she wiped your memory, those events should be gone. Even if she was dead, they shouldn't just come back by themselves. She must be somewhere which is suffocating her magic..."

Holly rubbed her head. "Sorry, I know this is all normal for you but I'm really having to lock my suspension of disbelief in the cupboard."

Roman smiled. "Oh, she'll stop banging on the door soon. I was the same way. If you like I can teach you some of the basics."

"I'm good just now, thanks."

Roman shrugged. "Alright. Well, you know where I am."

Holly gave him a thumbs up as she put her head down on the desk, ready to pass out.

"We have a room made up for guests. It's at the end of the hall."

"Thanks, Roman," she said, half-mumbling.

He slurped down the rest of his tea and left her to doze at the desk.

chapter 8

Within the cell, Arabella didn't get hungry or need to sleep. It had dual benefits for her jailers: they didn't need to interact with her or keep her running, and also it added to the sensory deprivation.

She didn't know how long she'd been in here. With no sun or moon through the little window, only an endless blanket of fog. Without her stomach telling her how long it'd been since her last meal. She could've been in here for days, or months. Lifetimes. She wasn't sure.

She had to get out of here. She knew that much. But her magic couldn't leave the cell, and no magic could get in. So, she couldn't even send a message to the Coven. Even if she could, she wasn't sure what she'd say. How she'd explain herself.

And the whole time, her stomach was gnawing with guilt and anxiety for Munro. Where was she? Was she okay?

She rattled the bars of her cell. "You can't just keep me in here forever!" she shouted, uselessly. She didn't know if anyone could even hear her. And anyway, it was a childish thing to think. Of course they could keep her in here forever. Who would stop them?

She sat in the corner of the cell and stared into space. There was nothing else to do. Her brain was starting to hallucinate shapes in the cell with her. Nonsensical monsters filled her vision as she became unsure whether she was awake or not. She tried to meditate, but her connection to the earth was so distant here.

"Hello, Ms. Morrow."

She knew the silvery voice without having to open her eyes. She didn't open them immediately. Like a child, it felt like she was somehow safer if she kept her eyes closed.

"Nicnevin," she said. "What can I do for you, your Majesty?"

"You can look me in the eye for a start. Unless you want to put even further disrespect on me than you already have."

Arabella opened her eyes.

Her heart quickened when she looked upon Nicnevin. She was so tall she stooped against the seven-foot-high ceilings of the corridor in which she stood. Her skin was a shimmering teal, what little light there was reflected off her as though she were underwater. Her hair was long and voluminous and raven black, her dress regal and dark blue-grey, like a rising storm cloud. One of her elegant hands ornamented a bar of Arabella's cell, revealing shining, beautiful black nails an inch long that could rip Arabella's throat out before she could even admire them.

Arabella tried to control her breathing. "Your Majesty," she said again.

Nicnevin smiled, her black lips revealing gleaming white teeth with sharp canines. "Don't play so coy with me. I told you, if I ever had to see you again, I would be the last thing you ever saw."

"Yes, I remember that." Arabella was tensed like a gazelle ready to run, except there was nowhere to go. "I'm not sorry though."

"I didn't think you would be," Nicnevin said.

"You said so yourself though, you won't kill me without a trial."

Nicnevin's fingers clenched around the iron bars of the cell, warping it. Her fury was nowhere on her face, but Arabella could feel it radiating off of her, like a typhoon on the horizon. It was quite a feat of strength for a fey creature to touch iron, let alone bend it.

"You just did the one thing that would ensure you will never make it out of the courtroom."

Arabella said nothing.

Nicnevin removed her hand, revealing the finger-marks now embedded in the iron. She looked around the cell, smiling. "Well, I hope it was worth it."

She turned to leave.

Before she vanished down the corridor, Arabella ran to the bars. "She was!"

Nicnevin turned, the true fury on her face now. It was only for a moment though, and then she turned and left.

Arabella sat back in her cell against the wall, heart pounding in her chest like she'd just had a near-death experience. And then she smiled.

She'd gotten under the Arch-Witch's skin.

"Gotcha."

chapter 9

Holly awoke after what could've been an hour or could've been twelve hours.

She sat up, looking around the Archive's guest bedroom. She was that groggy over-tired way where she just wanted to go back to bed.

The room was as eclectic as the rest of the house. All dark wood furnishings, the bed she'd been sleeping on was probably older than some countries. There was a clockwork astrolabe on the bedside table, gathering dust as it ticked, the planets revolving slowly around the sun. She checked her phone, which had seemingly charged itself overnight.

"Hm. I guess magic does qi charging now too," she said to herself, getting up and looking down at the spare pyjamas she'd been given that would've put Wee Willy Winkie to shame. Her discarded dirty clothes sat in a heap by the door. She poked her head out of the door and was hit by a waft of fry-up. Her stomach growled.

She padded out to the kitchen. Roman had an apron on, his shirt sleeves rolled up, and his big hair in a messy ponytail. He was heaping eggs, potato scone and square sausage onto plates. He laughed. "Mornin', sleepyhead. I thought that smell would get you up."

"Is that for me?"

"You get the full bed and breakfast treatment! Well, whenever I can be bothered."

"I assumed yous would all be vegan to be honest," Holly said, salivating as bacon and black pudding joined the growing plate.

"Iona and Arabella are. I just try to buy organic. I know, it's a sin."

"You'll get no complaints from me," Holly rubbed her hands together.

"May I say, those Ebenezer Scrooge pyjamas are very fetching," he said jokingly. She looked down at them again. There was an MC Hammer sag between the legs, and the previous owner appeared to have had something of a pot belly, as the stomach stretched out.

Holly laughed. "You know, they were actually quite comfy, all things considered."

"The previous owner thought so," Roman said.

Holly raised an eyebrow. "You didn't steal them, did you?"

"No, he died," Roman said matter-of-factly, before throwing the sizzling pan into the sink where it hissed until it went cold. When Holly blinked at him, he grinned. "That's right, you're wearing the pyjamas of a *dead man*." He gave an evil Dracula-esque laugh. "Och, relax! He died like two hundred years ago."

"How do you know what he thought about his pyjamas?"

Roman paused. "Do you want the true answer, or have you had enough magic stuff for one day?"

Holly didn't say anything.

"Just eat your breakfast." He picked up his plate, a knife and fork with one hand, and his book with the other. "I've got to go study. Make yourself at home!" he said, before dashing off back down the corridor that led to the bedrooms.

Holly picked at her food, suddenly weirded out all over again. For the archive, the mundane and the surreal seemed to blend together constantly and it was making her very uncomfortable.

As she ate the free breakfast, she considered just getting dressed and leaving, never coming back. But the thought put a deep pit in her stomach. Whatever had happened to Arabella, she had to find out. It wasn't even really about her own memories anymore. She was just worried. What sort of weird occult shit had she gotten herself into where even *these* lot were scared?

Polishing off her plate and doing the dishes for Roman, she went back to her room to find that her clothes had apparently washed, dried, and folded themselves into a neat pile where she'd left them. Next to them was a big fluffy towel.

She made to pick it up, when the towel lifted into the air by itself, swept across the room, and opened a door. The towel floated there as the door creaked open, revealing a little en-suite bathroom with a shower.

"Nuh-uh. Nope," she said, walking briskly from the room. She had the good sense to know that when a ghost invites you into the shower, you get the hell out of there.

***

She chapped Iona's door. The door opened by itself.

Iona was sitting at a large pedestal desk, strewn with papers. She was smoking a long tobacco pipe and writing in a large leather-bound volume. "What is it, dear?" She didn't look up, gaze fixed on her writing through the pince-nez glasses perched on the end of her nose.

"This is going to sound ridiculous," Holly said. "But no-one watches you in the shower here, do they?"

Iona looked up, completely taken aback. "I beg your pardon?"

"I, uh," Holly said, suddenly stumbling under Iona's piercing gaze. "Just, Roman had made it sound like there were ghosts floating around in here. And then when I picked up the towel, the bathroom door..."

A slow smile crept across Iona's face as she tried not to laugh. "No dear, no-one is watching. We actually have a lot of spectral defences on this house, you're safer here than you are in your own home."

"But the door—"

"We tell the towels to point out the showers for guests."

"Of course. That makes way more sense..."

If Iona picked up the sarcasm, she didn't react.

There was a banging from the main room. Iona shouted out. "Door!"

"I got it last time!" Roman shouted from his own room.

Iona rolled her eyes, tamping out her pipe and gathering her dress to stand up. "Excuse me, dear," she said, pushing past and heading down the corridor to the front door.

Holly sneaked a peek back at Iona's desk. She'd thought it would be a huge tome of spells or something, but it seemed to be some kind of ledger. *Books - £54. Sundries - £8.50. Tobacco - £10.*

She looked around and sure enough, a lot of the papers littered over the desk were receipts. The Tesco ones in particular looked a bit out of place among everything.

"Huh, I guess even being a witch doesn't save you from the dreaded accountancy," Holly said. She turned and went to find out who had been at the door.

***

Iona was comforting a teenage boy on the chair where Holly had been sitting herself not a few hours ago. He was tall and gangly, hair long and greasy, and he had his head in his hands. "I'm sorry, okay? I didn't know any better."

"Well, I'm not going to lie to you because frankly, it was a brainless thing to do," Iona said curtly, patting his back. "Now, tell me everything, and I'll see what we can do."

She looked up from him, seeing Holly in the doorway. "I'm afraid this is confidential, my dear. And did you not have a shower you were going to get to?"

"Uh, yeah. Sure. Right." A bit dazed, Holly started padding all the way up to her room again.

Did these people just run an inn for the supernaturally traumatised?

***

Drying her hair with the towel, Holly put her clean clothes on. They seemed like they were brand new again. She stretched, enjoying the feeling of the fabric on her clean skin. She'd definitely needed that.

Looking in the mirror, she tried to use her hands to make her hair stand up the way it usually did, but without at least a hairdryer she was getting nowhere. Besides, it seemed like everyone had too much to worry about to bother sourcing one for her.

She tiptoed back to the main room to find Roman perched on the periphery like an owl, watching Iona cross-examine the teenage boy.

"Him and his friends have some kind of club, they tried to trap a demon in a jar, and now his friend is possessed," he whispered, filling her in.

"I see…" Holly said.

"I was working on trying to find Arabella, but this seems like it needs to get dealt with right now."

"Okay, I think I have everything I need," Iona said conclusively, taking down the last of the information in her notebook. "I would recommend you stay with family for the time being. Is there anywhere else you can go?"

"Uh, yeah. Yeah. I'll go stay with my parents," he said, disoriented.

"Okay, we'll see you tonight, along with anyone else who was there when the demon was loosed. If you could arrange that?"

He nodded meekly.

"Lovely to meet you then. And, sorry. What was your name?"

"Charon," he said awkwardly.

Iona rolled her eyes. "Of course it is. Well, on your way. We have preparations to deal with." She led him out the door and closed it behind him. The bell on the door rattled behind it.

"We get two of these summonings a year these days. Today's supposed to be our day off! What happened to the Sabbath?" she muttered to herself. "Nothing's sacred anymore."

Roman cleared his throat. "I take it you need me to get the kit out?"

"Indeed. It's a fire demon, so be sure not to wear anything flammable, dear," she said. "I think it'll probably take all day to sanctify the space. He did it in a bloody church of all places. It'll be like trying to get rot off a corpse."

"Why is that?" Holly said.

Iona continued to rant as she moved round the room, piling up seemingly random objects.

"Churches are protected space," Roman filled in. "Sanctified. Like our house. Things can't get in. But that means if they do get in…"

"They can't get back out," Holly finished.

"Like trying to lead a fly out a window. We'll probably be there all night."

"Can I come?"

She wasn't even aware she was going to ask before the words were out of her mouth.

Roman smiled. "Getting a wee taste for it, eh? Oh, we'll make a witch of you yet, Holly doll."

"Call me Holly doll again and I'll knock you out."

Roman saluted. "Yes ma'am."

***

The exorcism wasn't until after the sun had gone down, so they'd sent Holly off while they prepared.

She'd ended up back home. Mostly because there was nowhere else she could think of going.

She sat on the couch in the now empty flat and stared at the flaking paint on the Artex ceiling.

She could just not go. Why had she asked to go? She didn't want to get involved in this.

Though, in her heart it seemed like she did.

She pulled her phone out, looked at the spider-web pattern cracked across the screen. As she poked it to make it do things, rainbow patterns skittered across the display under her touch.

And then it cut out.

She tried turning it back on, but nothing. It was broken.

A deep fear welled up in her as she thought about the money it would cost to get it fixed. But then the fear washed over her, and it was replaced by an empty feeling as she realised that she didn't immediately need to get it fixed.

She had no one to call.

Arabella was gone, off to wherever. And she'd been lying to her, or at least, deceiving her. These new folk probably didn't have phones.

She had no other real friends. Not one. She had workmates, a fragile web of acquaintances who slipped in and out of her life as it was convenient for her. None of them ever stuck around for long, but she'd thought she liked it that way.

She had no family — *they* had made that quite clear.

So it was just her. Her and Arabella in this mangy little flat, as she worked jobs she didn't care about, serving people she didn't like, until she was feeding the worms.

The image of the cyclist's skull bursting like a pustule as the tree grew out of it flew back into her mind, unsettling her stomach.

She went to the window, lit up a cigarette. She was going nowhere. Achieving nothing. Like a wheel spinning in muck, making nothing but mess.

If Arabella could hear her thinking like this though... The radical self-love of that bloody woman. She supposed, after everything they had been through, you either went one way or the other. Arabella's nuclear reactor of self-worth, or you turned into fucking Nietzche. Holly had chosen the latter. She couldn't be arsed with sunshine and rainbows.

She perched the cigarette on her lower lip to free her hand, so she could use both to crack the window open. They lived on a second floor flat, it made for good people-watching. Holly had spent hours smoking out this window over the last year, watching the people go about their lives. Opening the window fully, she hoisted her leg up and over, one foot on the brick outside, one in the comfy flat.

There was a little burn mark on the window-sill, and she poked at it with her finger. It was from...

Bella had chucked a throw pillow at her. It had knocked the cigarette out of her hand, and the pillow had gone tumbling into the street below.

She laughed, despite everything. Remembering Arabella flapping about, rushing down to get it.

Her life was a hundred billion of these little moments, layered on top of each other. Like a jumper the two of them had knitted together, woven so deeply it covered their shitty childhoods. She moaned about her life now, but she was lucky all things considered. Arabella's 'We Are All Miracles' chat was probably the right approach, as much as it made her eyes roll.

There was a twinge, she felt it. As she was turning this over in her mind, it was like her finger caught on another skelf, and she'd found another board covering a room in her brain.

She stubbed the cigarette on the exhaust pipe sticking out of the building wall and flicked it into the street as she turned it over in her head.

Arabella's font of self-worth, it came from somewhere. She'd said it a million times. They had sat on this very carpet, and she'd said...

Arabella and Holly, sitting legs crossed in the centre of the room. They'd pushed the coffee table out the way, and they were doing some kind of meditation.

Was Holly making this up? It had the ring of authenticity to it, she was sure. But she'd not once been interested in Bella's airy-fairy stuff!

... Had she?

"Bella, what you on about?" she'd asked.

"Holly, you have to keep it in your head at all times," Bella had smiled. *"We're Glasgow witches. There's none like us! The entire city out there is a generator that we can tap into all we need!"*

This didn't make any sense. The memory felt so disconnected from everything she knew. She could carbon date it — they'd only lived in this flat for a year and a half and it had definitely been right here. She moved and stood on the spot where they'd been sitting, as though it would trigger something.

Arabella had wiped this memory out of her brain. Someone had needed this covering up. But why?

She closed her eyes, and tugged on the thread, hoping it would unravel and not just snap.

What had happened next?

"Oh!" Arabella stood up, as the doorbell went. She snapped her fingers and there was a sparkle in the air. "Door's open!"

"Who's that?" Holly asked.

"It's— — —," Arabella said. Holly felt her brain strain as the details blurred and she searched for more. Even now though she could feel the

whole thing disappearing in her hands.

And then, the memory *changed*. She jumped, she noticed it this time. She'd been paying enough attention.

"It's PoDCasT BoYfRiEnd!" The new memory was acrid, obviously fake. It had a plastic smell to it and a chemical tint around it. But she might not have noticed under normal circumstances. She could feel herself wanting to just accept it.

Someone had walked into the room then. A person-shaped hole in the image of her mind. The entire memory was burned around them. Like someone had put their cigarette dout through the photo.

Arabella and Holly continued to talk as if there was nothing wrong. The person-shaped hole stood in the door, when they spoke it was just an unidentifiable mess. All Holly could remember was the tampered copy, and then the entire memory started to fracture around the Mystery Person, a splintering pane of glass.

She gasped, head pounding again.

But... it didn't add up. Roman had said, wherever Bella was, her magic was being suppressed. This didn't feel suppressed. This *wasn't Bella*. This had to be someone else. Someone else was altering her brain.

chapter 10

The sun went down halfway through the afternoon these days, so it wasn't much to say it was pitch-black out. They were dressed for the cold and standing on the street outside the church. The resplendent Gothic spire structure burnt black by the soot of industry which had long since left the city. It was beautiful — but no more so than any of the other three churches lining the main road. Every so often a car would drive past. Holly balled her hands into fists in her pockets, digging deeper to try and mine some heat out of the fabric.

"Are you sure we can't just burn the entire building down?" Roman said, putting his hands in his pockets and digging his chin into a thick tartan scarf.

Iona smiled faintly, looking up at the stained-glass windows. The Virgin Mary looked down on them, lit only by candlelight behind. For a second, Holly thought Iona hadn't heard. She was wearing one of those small Russian fur caps that framed her face and her cheekbones and covered her ears.

"Well, Roman, ignoring the fact that there's an irreplaceable human life in there who seems to be suffering… it's also a centuries-old, protected building." She looked back down at him and smiled, her dark eyes crinkling with something that Holly was not entirely sure was humour.

"Sorry I'm late," came a voice, as the greasy teenage boy slinked up the road. Charon? Was that his name? He didn't look like a Karen.

"I was beginning to think you'd chosen to stay home," Iona said. "Roman, if you could take Charon inside, I'd like to have a word with Holly before we go in."

Holly watched them leave and go up the stairs into the church, feeling like she was watching the lifeboats drift away.

"Honestly, I don't think this is a very safe place for you to be," Iona said, once they were out of earshot. "I just want to be certain you know that and give you a chance to leave. This has nothing to do with finding Arabella, and you don't owe us anything."

"No, I—" Holly said, her stomach tittering. "I feel like I've done all this before… I have memories of this world, and I need to unlock them."

Iona smiled. "Welcome to the path of the witch, my dear." She booped Holly's nose with a lapis-painted fingernail, making Holly aware how numb it was. "Knowledge is dangerous, but it's all we crave in this world. We can't ensure your safety, but we all look out for each other here. Do you understand?"

"Yes, ma'am," Holly said, and she found she meant it.

"Good. Now, keep your eyes open, your wits sharp, and be sure to listen to instructions. We're dealing with a demon. If he smells weakness, he'll pounce on it." And with that she put a hand on Holly's shoulder and led her into the old cathedral.

***

She'd expected it would be warmer than outside but somehow it got even colder. She felt her abdomen tense, against her will as the cold seeped through her clothes and into her bones.

Roman, who had been drawing some kind of markings on the doors, closed them as Iona and Holly entered.

Holly's breath fogged on the air. "I always forget how cold churches get. Those stone walls."

"It's not just that," Roman said. "He's a fire demon. He's nothing but heat. He's sucking it out of the rest of the building."

Charon was fidgeting, shifting his weight from foot to foot, looking around as if trying to find faces in dark corners.

"You mentioned the minister was here?" Iona said.

"Father Hardie," Charon nodded. "He's downstairs holding the door."

"Then we'll have to join him as quick as we can. I'm sure he's exhausted. Roman?"

Roman was pricking his finger with a knife, squeezing it like an orange and letting the blood pour on the marble tile floor. He drew his hand over the graffitied door, eyes closed and humming. He poured salt across the door, and the dripping blood started to soak into it, dyeing it pink.

"We are safe," he said aloud. *"This space is safe. It is sanctified. It is protected. So mote it be."*

Then he sat down with his legs crossed and began to breathe deeply.

Iona smiled. "That's the exits covered. Now, let's go catch a demon." She turned and began to walk down the steps as Charon indicated.

Holly hesitated. "I'll see you later, Roman." If he had heard her, he made no response, muttering chants under his breath in the dark.

***

"I can't hold it much longer," said a boy no older than sixteen, who had his hands against a thick wooden door at the bottom of the staircase. "Where the hell is he?"

"I'm here!" Charon shouted. "I got them!"

Holly came down the stairs gingerly, peeking ahead and trying to understand what she was seeing.

The young boy who had been holding both palms against the door was short, and lithe, and dark-skinned. His hair was curly, and revealed pointed ears, but his clothes looked perfectly average. Beside him, muttering prayers into a rosary, was the minister, an older man with tan skin that looked aged like leather.

"You've both done admirably," Iona said, sweeping to the front of them. "I am sorry to make you wait. My colleague has sealed the building, you can let go of the door."

She rested a hand on the boy's shoulder and arm, and he started to relax. His hands stuck as he started to pull them away, like he was scared to let go and he wouldn't let himself.

"Whatever's in there... I've never seen anything like it," the boy said. "We're in grave danger."

"We're always in grave danger, young man. But not to worry. That's why we're here." She gently removed his hands from the door. He breathed heavily, staring at it like it was about to burst open.

The priest lowered his rosary as he finished his current prayer. "You must be the witches."

Iona smiled. "The very same. Thank you for your hard work, Father. It's much appreciated."

"The creature in there is a stain that will never come out. But please, try and save the boy. He's an innocent in all this."

Iona wrung her hands in the cold. "I'll do my best."

Holly looked around the room, trying to understand what was going on. It almost felt like being an assistant to a wartime doctor in some old documentary.

The young boy collapsed into Holly's arms.

"Duncan!" Charon shouted, as Holly stumbled to keep her balance, lowering to the ground with him and resting him.

"That's a considerable amount of magic for a young fairy to extend for all this time," Iona said. "Charon, you may want to go get him something with a lot of sugar and caffeine in it."

"A fairy..." Holly said to herself. The boy's features definitely *looked* elven. The torchlight shone on his skin, reflecting on strong cheekbones and the pointed ears. He stirred, like he was having a nightmare.

Iona turned to Father Hardie. "I don't usually mix practices when I'm doing one of these, so I will ask you to stay outside to begin with? I'll be sure and scream if I need you. You focus on these young wards of yours."

Father Hardie nodded. "May God help you."

Iona smiled wickedly. "I'm sure she'll be watching." Then she looked at Holly expectantly. "Holly! The door please!" And she nodded to the door they'd been protecting.

As Holly approached the door, Iona raised her hands as though bracing for an impact, muttering an incantation under her breath.

Holly put a hand on the brass doorknob, and as it hissed she pulled her hand back. "Ow!" She looked at her hand, red and scorched like a blister ready to form. "It must be really hot in there," she said.

"It's a fire demon, Holly," Iona said, with none of the warmth from earlier. "Chop, chop."

Holly pulled her sleeve up over her hand, and wrapped it, covered, round the doorknob.

In one fluid motion, she turned the knob and the door flew open. She backed up at the wave of humid, thick heat which flooded the room.

"In!" Iona shouted, grabbing Holly around the torso and pulling them both in. She swung her hand, and the door slammed closed behind them.

***

The inside of the room was hot, stiflingly so. The humidity clung to Holly's face, stuck in her lungs. The stone church walls were dripping with condensation and lit only by a few small braziers on the wall. An ancient prison cell that was probably a thousand years old.

The boy in the corner couldn't have been older than sixteen. He cowered, sleekit, in the corner, a shaggy mat of brown hair hanging over eyes wide and fearful, like a deer with its foot in barbed wire. He was drenched with sweat and trying not to look at them directly. There was blood on his shirt, on his fingernails, and scratch marks across all the walls.

Iona stood tall, somehow. Holly felt a deep urge to run from somewhere in her brain beyond logic. She was in danger. Escape. Get out.

She smothered the feeling.

Iona took a deep breath and addressed the boy. "You're doing a good job holding him in. He seems very powerful."

"Please," he said. His voice croaked, like he'd been screaming himself hoarse. "Get him out."

"We will. But we need to speak to him."

"If I let go now, I'll fall apart. I'll never find my way back up." He squeezed his skull like he was trying to push his brain out of it.

"We'll catch you," Iona said, and she took a step forward. A sign of trust.

Holly couldn't help it, she ducked in behind Iona like a shield. She didn't need magic. She could feel it, radiating off of him. There was a parasite in that boy that wanted to choke the life out of her. She was starting to sweat, and pant in the heat.

Matthew mewled in the corner, almost as though they weren't even there. "No, no, no... He's toying with me. You can't."

"I speak now to the being who has made its nest in the soul of Matthew Moon," Iona said, as though an incantation.

"He doesn't wanna..." Matthew said. "He knows what you're here for. He's not coming out." He looked at her then, right in the eyes. Gaunt cheeks and fear in his eyes like Holly had never known.

"Is that maybe a sign?" Iona said. "That I can help get him out of you?"

"Impossible," he said. "We're one person now. He's eaten me."

"No that's not true, Matthew. No matter what lies he's put in your head, no matter how he's twisted you... you're still a human being."

Matthew stared at her, fear giving way to a blankness. Looking at her like she was a newspaper in a language he didn't read.

"What is he saying to you, Matthew?"

His upper lip curled back over his teeth as he smiled. "None of your business, witch." He'd stopped shivering.

"I assume I am talking to the demon inside?" Iona said, unwavering.

Matthew peered round Iona, looking at Holly with that blank, empty stare. Like a tiger watching a child walk past its cage. He licked his chops.

Iona snapped her fingers, drawing his attention. "Demon. What is your name?"

"I am Dark Moon," he said, absently. "I am Matthew's inner, essential wickedness." He smiled, before going back to watching Holly.

Just his eyeline was aggressive. Holly squirmed under that unblinking gaze. Something was wearing that boy's face like a mask. It tugged on his facial muscles like a puppeteer, approximating human movements but the grip was too tight. When he smiled the eyes were too wide, the lips too parted, the jaw too tight and yet the teeth, slightly too open.

"You've brought me a wee lamb," he added, as though Iona was no longer in the room.

"You are not this boy, that lie you've told him won't work on me," Iona said.

Holly heard the drip of condensation on the floor, tried to control her breathing. This thing was inside that boy, and she was feeling this just standing near him.

"I am Matthew's deepest soul, his guilt and fear and sin," the demon said, his voice now slippery as a fish. And then he screamed, as Iona threw a handful of salt into his face, and it turned to fire on his skin.

He rattled in the chains, wracked with pain. "Uppity witch!" he shouted. "So desperate to save the boy... But you couldn't save your wife, could you?"

She threw another handful of salt in his face, and he screamed. The torches in the room flared as he did. Matthew's fingers and body twisted into unnatural shapes as he screamed, his bones cracking as his skin bubbled like soup.

He laughed through the screaming, and when it died down, he said, "You're just hurting the boy. This vessel is his, I care not what you do to it."

"I thought you were one and the same," Iona said.

He looked at her, caught in the lie.

He said nothing, instead craning his neck to look at Holly. "Come closer, wee lamb."

Iona reached back and took Holly's hand, not taking her eyes from the demon for a moment. "She's fine where she is." She squeezed the hand.

The demon laughed, a low rattling laugh like he had rubble in his lungs. Her fear was giving him strength.

Holly thought of that wee boy in there, with his skin worn like a suit, and another instinct rose in her. This one not primal but learned. A defence mechanism.

She stepped forward, chest out, chin up. "Listen mate, me and Iona are gonna pull you out of that kid if we have to cut you into ribbons to do it."

He laughed again. "Oh, there it is! The rage of a Glasgow witch."

"Name yourself," Iona said, squeezing Holly's hand again.

"But what is that inside you, I wonder?" the demon continued, looking at her. Through her. As though Iona wasn't even there. "You have so much magical potential, but no defences."

"Name yourself, demon!"

"It's like you've had it all boarded up in your brain," the demon's eyes flickered like he was reading her. Like her brain was a textbook to be leafed through. She could feel him probing at her mind but covering her head did nothing to keep him out.

Iona threw another handful of salt at the demon's chest and Matthew screamed again, his neck tendons tightening like cables but his eyes, feral, wouldn't leave Holly.

"*What is your name, demon?*" Iona shouted.

"Arson!" he blurted out, tongue compelled. But he wasn't even looking at her. He licked Matthew's tongue over teeth encrusted by maggots, and the smell of rancid piss filled the room as a wet patch dribbled down his leg.

Holly retched at the smell.

The demon cackled. "I wonder, wee lamb. It would not be beyond the skill of a demon like me to tease out that power..."

Bile rose up Holly's throat, and she punched him square in the jaw. Iona put her hand up to stop her. "Don't. You're not hurting him. You're just hurting the child. He's winding you up, it tightens his grip."

This close, she could smell the burning flesh from the salt wounds. His body stank of piss and barbecued flesh. She could see the heaving in Matthew's chest as Arson animated him like a marionette.

"Besides," Iona said. "We have what we need now."

His gaze flicked, with sudden visceral anger, to Iona. Looking at her for once. "Damn you, woman."

"With defiance and grit, with patience and wit,
We wrest this creature from its pit,
And trap its soul, binding it!"

Iona raised her hands, casting the spell. The rattling chains pulled taut as Matthew was lifted into the air. "With me!" she shouted to Holly, who pulled out the scrap of paper Iona had given her with the rite on it.

She opened her mouth and recited her first spell.

"We call your name!
We shun, and shame!
The truth beneath your lying mask!
Witches of old, we humbly ask!
Lend us your love! Lend us your power!
Come to us in this vital hour!
Leave this boy, leave him be!
By naming you, we compel thee!"

Iona dumped the remainder of her salt over Matthew's head. The torches flared into infernos as the demon flailed against the chains, trying to fly into the air.

"Arson!" Iona shouted. *"I name you, Demon of fire!"*

The inferno died down, and all was silent for a moment, but the dripping of condensation down the walls continuing. Drip, drip.

They watched Matthew fall to the ground in a heap, Iona's hand gripping Holly's like a vice.

Matthew lay in a ball, shivering. Holly went to move forward, but Iona stopped her. "Not yet..."

Holly, hand out, felt a drip on her hand. And another.

She pulled it back, and looked at it in the dark. It was viscous, dark. Wine red.

She looked up.

The entire ceiling was matted with thick, dripping blood.

And then the banks burst. Holly covered her head with her hands, but there was no way to stop it, they were drenched. In her face, on her clothes, the coppery taste of it in her mouth, and then she slipped on the wet sticky floor and spread it around even more.

She looked out to Matthew, curled in a ball, now dyed red by it. He lifted his head up, gripping his chest like something was squeezing his heart, making noises like he was winded. He retched, eyes bulging, as she saw something thick and protruding making its way up his tract.

Iona, hands and fingers slippery, struggled with pulling a jar from her jacket pocket, unscrewing the cap. "Here he comes!"

Matthew's neck swole as the lump rose out of it, and then he wheezed as fountains of smoke burst from his mouth, from his nose, like a ruptured artery.

The smoke collected against the ceiling, probing for an escape, but golden light sparked at the walls — Roman and the others' spell was holding — and it swirled, like a pacing lion in a cage.

Dropping the jar to raise both her hands, Iona threw up a shield of golden light right as the demon smoke pounced. The jar hit the ground, luckily bouncing rather than smashing.

"Open the jar!" Iona shouted, pushing the shield to try and keep the demon back.

Holly grabbed it, fingers slick with blood, but it wouldn't turn, and she could see the smoke starting to creep around the edges of the shield. She grabbed her t-shirt, trying to wrap the inside around it to get a better grip but the shirt itself was also soaked, and she could feel the demon around her like whispers as the smoke started to seep into her ears, her nostrils, her eyes, filling her lungs...

"Iona!" she shouted.

Iona turned, raising a hand, but before Holly could see what happened, the darkness covered her eyes completely, and then there was nothing.

chapter 11

Holly was in the dark. All she could see, for miles around. She could've been at the bottom of ocean. Or in deep space. She reached her hand out but there was nothing outside of her own body.

"You haven't been down here in a while, have you?"

She turned. Standing behind her, with her hands in her pockets, was herself. The same red hair, the same tatty jeans and leather jacket she'd been wearing. The same brown eyes she'd always thought were so boring. But there was something different about her. It was the same instinctive revulsion she'd felt looking at Matthew. Something behind the eyes.

The Other Holly smiled. It was a genuine smile, but it held no warmth.

"Where are we?"

"Welcome to your twisted mind, kid," the Other Holly said, rolling her eyes. "You know I liked the other one, but you're definitely more my fit."

Holly's hands balled into fists, knuckles white. "Get out of my head."

"See what I mean? You've got something of the fire about you too. Stubborn. Principled. Angry."

"You have no idea how angry I can get," she said.

"That intimidating mask works less well when I can hear everything going on in here," the Other Holly tapped her temple. "Besides, what are you going to do? Punch me again?"

She did. Her hand passed right through the Other Holly, and she dissipated like smoke, swirling away like sand scattering from a stone dropped in a lake.

"No, no, no! Bonehead!" the Other Holly said. She was behind her again. "This is your mind, what would that even mean! Useless!"

She felt a sudden muscle weakness, stumbling to her knees as though she'd run a marathon. Her limbs were heavy, she heaved.

"It's too *easy*... I thought you'd put up more of a fight but you're like a raw nerve. You have so much magic but it's like you've forgotten even the most basic training!"

Holly heaved, too out of breath to speak. What the hell was he talking about? The Other Holly — this demon, Arson — was draining her energy. She wondered suddenly what was happening outside. In the actual world. Iona and Roman would have to be doing a second exorcism because of her mistake.

"Not a mistake," the Other Holly smiled, bending down and grabbing her by the scruff of the neck. "A deficit. You're empty inside. No passion flows in your veins, and I know. Because I'm nesting in your heart now."

Holly heaved, retched. Like her body was trying to reject the demon. The Other Holly laughed.

"This is your life now. You're a vehicle."

Holly shook her head. "No."

The Other Holly smirked. "No?"

Holly smiled back. "No. I don't know what I want from life, yet. But I know what I don't want. And I will *never* stop fighting you."

There was a murmuring across the darkness. At first Holly thought it was just the wind, but then she realised she could hear voices from outside. Shouting. Roman and Iona. And what sounded like others. Holly grinned. "Sounds like the cavalry's coming."

The Other Holly was looking off in the distance, furious.

"You're right," Holly said. "I haven't been down here in a while. But I spent most of my teenage years down here. And I always found my way out."

Suddenly, the colour flooded back in, the image before her vanished as the world rushed in to fill the darkness.

She was back in the room in the dingy little church, floating four feet in the air. Roman, Iona, and the young elf boy were chanting in a circle, bigging her up. Pulling the demon back on the other end.

"You are so tiny, little demon," Holly said, swallowing as she sensed the place the demon sat in her chest. Oh, this was gonna hurt.

She didn't have any idea where the knowledge came from. It was instinct, or a past life. Something.

She reached a hand into her own chest and wrenched Arson out of her. Fire erupted from her, lapping up her hand, catching on her jacket, she screamed, and ripped her hand up, pulling the demon out in one swoop.

It burned in her hand, a little ball of depleted plasma. She pulled it up and looked at it as she lowered to the ground and the chanting came to an end.

A small face, pathetic in the light of day, started to form on the plasma's surface.

"Your hand should be burning..." it said, voice small and hissing like a gas leak.

"I have some of that fire inside me, remember?" Holly said to it. "You don't get to decide what my limits are."

Iona was holding out the mason jar, standing as well back as she could. Holly dropped it in, and it fell to the bottom as Iona screwed the cap on. As the oxygen in the jar burned up, it grew dimmer, and bluer, and its face disappeared.

Roman whooped, "Well done hen! Where'd you learn how to do that?"

Holly felt her knees start to give out, but she steadied herself.

Iona grabbed her in a huge hug with the hand free from holding the mason jar. "Oh, my dear, I am so sorry. That was far too dangerous, I led you into the lion's den."

Holly patted Iona on the back. "No. Thank you." She couldn't quite put her finger on why, but she felt more alive than she had in a very long time.

***

"We'll deal with the demon, banish it somewhere it'll not get back from for a long time," Iona said at the front door of the church, still holding the mason jar like it was radioactive.

"Thank you, ma'am," said Father Hardie. "I'll make sure the weans don't get involved in anything as dangerous as that again. You've got my thanks."

Charon and the fairy, Duncan, were standing looking very sheepish next to him.

"See that you do," Iona said.

"And for the record?" Roman said. "Running a Black Magic Club out of a church? Very weird."

"It's a long story," Father Hardie said.

"Let's go," Iona said to Roman and Holly, and they stepped off the church grounds just as the sun came up.

As they started the trek back to the Archive, Roman stared at the demon in the flask, watching it undulate like a lava lamp. "I still can't believe you managed to pull that thing out yourself. I was a little worried when it possessed you, but you've got a bright career as a witch ahead of you."

Holly blushed. "I don't know about that. I did have help."

"No, he's not wrong," Iona said. "Even with help, the ability to exorcise a demon from yourself? It's a skill people need years of practice for."

Holly's face burned, and she remembered what the demon had said — something about forgetting her training. But she was eager to get herself off the hot seat, so she asked, "So what do we do with it now? Do you just have a cupboard of these jars gathering dust somewhere?"

"Oh, God no. What if one of them got out?" Iona said. She lifted it up, looking at it under the crisp morning light. "We're going to need a very big circle to banish it."

chapter 12

"Arabella..." came a voice, as Arabella was just starting to drift off into something that was as close to sleep as she would get in Elf-hame. She started, disoriented, casting around.

Her focus came as she looked at the bars. It was Munro. Her heart melted.

"Oh, Munro..." she said, rushing to the bars. "Where have you been? Have they hurt you?"

Every time Arabella saw Munro, she fell in love all over again. She'd never felt this way for anyone before. She'd been in *love*, but... with Munro it was different. Like every time she looked at her it was like looking into the sun, she had to look away or her eyes would burn. Tall, broad, her selkie coat wrapped around her. Her eyes, pale blue and distant, and her face, usually pale as sea foam, though now flushed red with exertion.

Arabella rushed to the bars, tried to put her hands through them to touch Munro's. To feel her strong calloused fingers, to be enclosed and safe. But of course, the magic on the cell stopped her. The distance felt like it spanned oceans.

"I came as quickly as I could, my love," Munro said, looking back up the corridor. "They could be back any minute. I had to see you though."

"What's going on out there?" Arabella said. "I've not been able to get in contact with anyone."

"Nicnevin's taking you to the Seelie Court," Munro said. "She's putting you to death, and having my memories wiped."

"She can't do that!"

"Honestly, I don't think we can stop her," Munro said, her eyes welling up. "She won't even see me like this. We've really pushed it too far this time."

"Fuck 'too far'!" Arabella said. "I love you, and anything short of spending my entire life with you is not far enough."

Munro laughed through tears. "Bella, my beautiful witch..." She put her hand up to touch Arabella, and Arabella did the same. An invisible wall of force stood between them. "How will I count the days without you?"

"You won't. Not for a long time, anyway. I'm going to get Nicnevin back for this, and you're going to get your freedom."

"But—"

"But nothing," Arabella said. "She's messed with the wrong witch."

Munro smiled. "Stop doing that, you're too fucking beautiful when you're angry."

Arabella laughed. "I've missed you."

"I've missed you too my love."

Arabella closed her eyes and reached out with her mind, trying to feel Munro on the other side of the bars. Flexing every fibre of magic in her being against the cage, she spoke:

"With plaintive cries and death on our tails,

Love carries us, the wind in our sails,

The witch and the selkie, the outcome's unclear,

We forge our own path to the future from here."

Arabella opened her eyes and took a deep breath. Munro was watching her with that loving look in her eyes that always made her feel like she was going to burst.

"Did it work?" Munro asked. "Your spell?"

Arabella smiled. "You never know straight away. But you live in hope. Come back as soon as you can, I'll work out something more concrete. I'm not just rotting in this jail cell until they put me down like an animal."

Munro nodded.

She stayed by her side, as long as she could possibly get away with, maybe a bit longer than that, before slinking off as the next guard changed his shift.

Arabella watched her go and felt the spell taking root in her own heart. The magic of these bars was nothing. She was patient. She was strong. She just had to keep going.

chapter 13

The Glasgow Subway is an underground metro system that has been running more or less continuously since 1896. It is formed of two concentric circles which go in opposite directions of each other — the Inner and Outer Circles — bisecting the River Clyde which Glasgow is built around.

A few of the names of the stations have changed in its century and a quarter of service, but only one station was ever closed completely. The Merkland Street station, which was completely demolished and replaced with the enormous Partick interchange station a few metres away. You can still see the hump of the old tunnel.

It was there, under cover of night, that the Coven of Merchant City stood between the Morrison's and Partick subway station, and Iona handed Roman the jar with the demon in it to free up her hands.

"Keep edgy," Roman warned, nudging his nose at Holly, who

looked up and down the street for anyone who might be wandering past.

"What are we doing here?"

"We're sending little Arson here back to hell. Or wherever he came from," he tapped the little jar, as Iona pulled a broom from behind her back and started to sweep, as though she was trying to find something under the road dust on the pavement.

"Why do we have to do it here?"

"There's a really good spot here to break into the Underground network."

Holly looked up at the Partick building behind her. "You don't mean like, the Underground underground?"

Roman raised an eyebrow. "Do you know a bigger circle in this city?"

Suddenly Holly remembered the memories Arabella had wiped again. Standing at that crossroads, soaking in the energies of the city...

"I think I'm starting to understand," she said.

Roman grinned, and his eyes glinted. In the darkness he looked quite mad. "You're seeing the Matrix."

She snorted. "Stop that."

"Glad to have you as part of the team. Welcome aboard," Roman nudged her with his elbow.

"Got it," Iona said, interrupting them. She pawed at a little groove in the pavement, and as the dust came away, it was revealed to be a little intricate sigil, carved with some kind of chisel.

She drew a chalk circle around it, and stood, one hand raised so her index finger touched her nose.

"City old, with creaking bone,
We require your aid, we require your might.
Ancient foundation hewn of stone,
Reveal your entrance for this rite."

The rune on the ground lit up and began to expand. As it did, the stone beneath seemed to push out like interlocking pieces in a puzzle, sliding away to reveal an opening.

Iona stepped back as the magic locked into place, and now there was a staircase leading down into the bowels of the subway.

"Come along, loves," she said, taking the demon jar from Roman and using it as a lamp to lead the way.

*****

It definitely smelled like the Subway, Holly thought. That clammy, sulfuric humidity that suffused all the tunnels. It used to fog her glasses, when she'd worn them, and it clung to her clothes and her hands.

This tunnel wasn't polished and lit and colourful though and, as they descended, she honestly could've believed they were walking into hell itself.

They walked for a few minutes in a winding pattern. Left and right, and sometimes up a little, but trailing inevitably downwards towards wherever Iona was leading them by the light of the captured demon.

Eventually they came out into the back of a long room that was familiar. The dilapidated remains of the Merkland Street station, exactly like the reconstruction she'd seen in the Transport Museum as a little girl. Unlit, unmanned, with a section of the ceiling caved in and cobwebs lining the walls, it had an eerie quality. You could almost feel the people who had walked around in it before it had closed down.

Roman put his backpack down on the ground and pulled out a number of candles.

Iona handed the jar to Holly. "Would you like to lead?" she asked. "You're the one who pulled it out after all."

"Are you sure? This all seems very dangerous."

"The only way you learn is by doing, I've found," Iona said. "And I sense that you want to learn."

Holly felt an unsureness wriggling in her stomach. "How can you tell?"

"I just can. You gain a way of noticing others like yourself." The older woman, hands now free again as Holly took the jar, tied her long raven hair in an elastic bauble.

Holly looked inside the jar. She couldn't deny it. Now that the evidence was directly in front of her, she felt an urge to chase this knowledge. And more than anything, she wanted to send this thing somewhere very far away.

"Alright," she said, eventually, as Roman started to light the candles, and the ghostly room began to flicker with the dim glow of the fire light.

"Close your eyes," Iona said. "And attune to the energy of the circle."

Holly closed her eyes, and took a deep breath, inhaling the egg-like stench of the tunnel. It opened her memories like a book. The first time she'd been in here that she could remember, she'd been eight years old. She'd ridden the underground multiple times a week through her teen years, from direct travel to using it to connect the bus routes.

Arabella was right, now that she thought of it. It was like being inside the city's circulatory system. She imagined them all, the people walking around like blood cells, carrying their own problems and triumphs, their lives shuttling around as they went to and fro, unaware of the city breathing in and out.

The thick wall of the subway smell was pierced by the tang of an incense, and she opened her eyes to find Roman was burning some.

"Let's do this," Roman said.

Iona nodded, and the three of them stepped into the tiny circle of candles, a microcosm of the subway, and closed hands with each other, the jar in the centre of them.

***

Iona raised her hands as the three of them chanted, Holly barely managing to follow the words as she tried to guess the end of each line.

A circle of lights fizzed into existence around them, sparkling like fireworks in yellow and pink and green. With a sweep of Iona's hand, half of them shot off up one of the tunnels in one direction, and then with another sweep, the other half flew in the other direction.

"Follow them," she said, taking the others' hands again, rocking gently back and forth.

Holly could feel them, if she thought about it enough. She watched as though floating above them, passing under the city unseen. Eastwards towards the city centre, across the Clyde, and back along the South Side. And the others, in reverse. The people, sleeping in their beds as they moved like whispers.

These tunnels had power. It was like Arabella had said. She could feel the ghosts of people bustling around, the circulation. Six hundred thousand lives, each buzzing with their own complexity, but collectively? Collectively the care they imbued on their piece of the world hummed through the mortar, through the bricks, through the metal and concrete jungle, carrying it like a circuit.

They were drawing on the whole city now. Round and round and round they went like a Catherine wheel on Guy Fawkes'. Above their heads, a storm raged.

"You are not welcome here demon," Roman said, breaking the chant, and Holly jumped. She hadn't realised she'd still been going. "You, fiend, will be cast back. So sayeth us. Do not darken our plane again. So mote it be."

"So mote it be," they repeated.

The jar between them began to... twitch. Wriggle. It rattled.

The gushing wind around them rose to a fever pitch, and Holly realised it was the sound of the trains coming. Down both tunnels at the same time. The tiny little trains that make tourists laugh, because despite their size they *roar* like jungle cats.

"Carry this spirit from us, and never again may it return!"

The sound of the trains grew louder, and louder, Holly's lungs overfilling as the trains compacted the air in the platform, the pounding under their feet shaking the jar ever harder, until it tipped—

And shattered on the ground.

The others didn't flinch. Arson, burst from his cage, floating up, arms akimbo, twisting.

Iona and Roman gripped Holly's hands on either side, their circle holding him in.

"By the power flowing through this city, begone demon!"

The demon threw a fist, striking an invisible barrier—

Holly felt a lurch, saw in her mind's eye as the Squinty Bridge, up on the Clyde, heaved and creaked to one side. Without thinking, she reacted, swiping her hand forward—

The Bridge twisted round and, somehow, hit Arson across the sternum. He smarted, coughing, and Iona looked at her, with a glimmer of surprise, before swinging her hand back, and striking into the circle—

Glasgow Green tumbled over him like a wave, the soil filling his mouth as he screamed, fingers pushing hopelessly against the tide before the greenhouse...

Holly wouldn't know how to draw what she was seeing. These things were happening, visibly, in front of her, but she also knew that if she was standing up there right now, she wouldn't be able to see it. Like space had warped and become fluid, and in this circle, all things were possible.

Roman took a deep breath, gathering power between his hands, and then, exhaled like a dragon.

The neighing and whinnying of horses, and a statue of a man on a horse with a traffic cone on his head came galloping towards them, colliding with Arson and knocking him this way and that inside the bubble they'd trapped him in.

"You are not welcome here!" Iona shouted, starting a chant, and they repeated, "Your hatred is not welcome here!"

Arson tensed, taking a deep breath, and Holly was sure he was about to simply vanish, when he released, and two jets of fire broke the bubble and collided with Iona and Roman. They tumbled to the floor, their clothes singed, and didn't get up.

Arson stretched, free to move now, and looked at Holly like a prawn cocktail on a fancy platter.

"What's your plan now, little baby-witch?" he said, smiling.

Her heart was jackhammering in her chest. She could feel her fear rejuvenating him.

"I've been in your head. I know your limits. Bow before me, witchling, and I may just let you live."

No. That wasn't how this worked. She knew that. She'd been in his head as well.

"I bow before no-one!" she shouted. She could feel the circuit under her, still humming with power. If she could just... "You are not welcome! In my home? In my city?"

Arson's face twinged with unexpected fear, as he realised she'd pushed him onto the train tracks.

"But you can't..." he started.

She didn't even speak. She swung a fist—

The Necropolis—

Brought her hand up—

The Rennie Mackintosh House—

Kicked out with her foot—

The Glasgow Cathedral, and behind it, the hundreds of holy buildings, stretching back from now into a thousand years in the past. Every prayer of thanks, every communion, and every drop of blood spilled over their banks in the name of sectarianism.

History. She was using their history. Their shared history, on this one spot. Together, they defied entropy. They defied the universe. What was a demon to them?

Arson screamed, buffeted by the oncoming winds. The trains were getting louder.

She gathered energy in her hands, and struck Arson with them—

The thousands of ships on the Clyde, the generations of men who'd made their livelihoods, fed their weans on that river. The life-giving water that had flown through their home for millennia before they'd even arrived.

Arson twisted, turned, tried to get away but he was pinned now, pinned by the city, the jagged buildings encroaching above him like the teeth on a steel trap, closing as Holly pulled them all around.

She couldn't finish it, she realised. She was starting to flag. She didn't have the energy. Her legs were like jelly.

And then she felt a hand on her shoulder. She turned her head. Roman was beaming. "Keep it goin', hen. Well done." Behind him, Iona was still getting to her feet.

The entire subway lit up with lights. The ground around them was shaking. Above, the streetlights flickered as the circle drew all the power of the city into one point. The screaming of the spectral trains of a hundred-and-twenty-five years going round and round, and round and round.

Arson was being crushed as they circled and circled like vultures. "Wait! Wait! Just wait! We can make a deal!"

"No chance," Holly said, and clapped her hands together.

A bolt of lightning passed round the circle, and the power collapsed into a point. A tear in the fabric of reality, through this one point she could see everywhere.

Arson grasped and pulled at the edges.

"No! No!" Arson said. "Let me go!" But there was no fighting the gravity of a universe.

She could see behind the portal... A tree, a vast tree connecting everywhere. There were the hells, where Arson would end up, and there was...

Through a vast fog, her mind's eye flew across the expanse. Flying like an eagle, homed in on her target, she travelled thousands of miles in an instant to reach—

Arabella turned in her cell. "Holly?" She looked right at her.

Arson was swallowed, and the portal closed behind him.

And then the adrenaline ran out, and Holly keeled over.

chapter 14

Whittling, whittling, whittling away.

Two stones, she'd picked from around the cell. They had a nice size, and weight in the hand. Good for crafting.

Arabella wasn't quite sure how long she'd been sitting in that one spot, dragging one stone along the other. She'd labelled one the whetstone and the other the one she was going to sharpen, but it was more or less arbitrary. She was going to flatten it into a perfect disc, polished to a shine.

Magic, like excellence, was a habit. By pure focus, she was going to will this into existence whether there was an anti-magic field around the cell or not.

Nothing else mattered. It provided a nice distraction at any rate. Like a marathon, she wasn't thinking about the end. Just polishing, sharpening, and allowing her mind to wander.

Something stirred, and she perked up. She turned, and something crashed into her like a cresting wave on the beach—

It was Holly. Standing on some kind of train platform in the dark. Wait, was that the Merkland Station they did exorcisms in?

"Holly?" she asked, out loud.

Holly was looking right at her. She seemed to open her mouth but then—

The vision faded, Holly's astral form zipping back up the World Tree.

What on Earth was going on back there?

She picked up the stones, which she'd dropped on the ground, and renewed her work.

chapter 15

Holly's eyes flickered open. Roman and Iona were standing over her and, for a second, she thought she was still on the platform before she realised she was lying on something soft. She sat up to see she was on the couch back at the Archive.

"Oh my god, she's alright..." Iona said, when she saw her regain consciousness, turning away.

"You did good, hen," Roman said, smiling. "Socked him right in the gut!"

"Yeah, no thanks to you," Holly smiled, pushing herself up into a sitting position with a grunt.

Roman looked crestfallen. "Yeah, we're really not living up to the hype, are we?"

"Oh no I didn't mean that!" Holly rushed. "Just, I'm. I don't know. I'm glad you're okay."

"Aw, it'll take more than a demon to knock us down. Though he might have managed it if you hadn't been there. We're strongest as a trio, usually. Without Arabella it's…"

"Arabella!" Holly remembered. Iona was staring out the front windows, distracted by something. "I saw her!"

"What?"

"When we banished the demon! I got a flash of her in my head!"

Iona turned, eyes wide. "You're telling me you managed to hold back that demon on your own, *and* reached out through the breach to see Arabella with True Sight?"

"I… I don't know what that means, but yes?"

"My dear, I think you might just have the makings of a very powerful witch inside you if you apply yourself. I was already thinking it when you managed to hold it back without our help, but…"

"Where was she?" Roman interrupted. "Arabella! Where did you see her?"

"She was…" Holly thought back. There had been so little detail. "She looked like she was in a jail cell. There was a thick fog."

"Well, it doesn't sound like one of the nine hells," Roman said to Iona. "That's a good sign."

"Hm," Iona looked crestfallen. "If she's where I think she is, she's in a lot of trouble indeed."

***

"The Land of Elf-hame," Iona said, as she coaxed an image into the space around them. "It's almost as big as our own world."

"I'm sorry, Elphame?" Holly said.

"Yes, Elf-hame." The image began to solidify into a large tree in front of them. Large and wide-reaching, old and knotted and whorled.

"Elf-hame is a tree?"

"No, no, this is the universe."

Holly raised an eyebrow. "Like, the World Tree? Like the Norse thing?"

"You know, pop culture has a tendency to warp everything, but it does save on a lot of the explanations," Iona said. "If you'd prefer you can look at it this way—"

She snapped her fingers and the image rearranged itself into a large web with strands that reached into infinity.

She snapped again — neurons firing in a brain, a nervous system.

And again. Planets revolving around stars, revolving around galaxies.

"They're all parts of the whole. Different interpretations of limited data. Different ways of understanding the cosmic infinity of our beautiful universe."

Holly looked at her with a smirk. "You've given this speech before, haven't you?"

Iona blushed, uncharacteristically, taking a drag of her pipe to buy her a moment. She waved her hand across the image, and it dissolved back to the spider web view. "Anyway," she said. She reached into the image with both hands and pulled it out like revealing a cat's cradle. "If we're looking for a land in the universe, not on our plane, which is shrouded in a continual fog..."

The zoom got larger and larger, until the fog surrounded them, filled the whole room.

Holly looked around, behind her. She couldn't see a foot in front of her face. "Arabella's here?"

"Somewhere. I assume," Iona said.

"What a horrible place to live," Holly said.

"That's a bit judgmental," Roman said, waving his hands and dispelling the fog. The room, by contrast, seemed brighter, warmer than before. "You know there are probably people who think that about where you live."

"Nah," Holly smiled. "I live in the best city in the world."

Roman shook his head, scoffing. "You sound like Arabella."

"Well, speaking of Arabella," Iona said. "Perhaps now that we can guess where she is, we can Scry her."

"And she knows we're looking for her," Roman said. "At least from the sound of it. So maybe she'll be easier to pinpoint." Roman was already crossing the room. "Do we have any maps of Elf-hame?"

"No," Iona said.

He stopped. "What?"

"The place moves around, shifts like tectonic plates. You can't map it traditionally. And any map you tried to create with magic would be far too complicated for a simple Scrying spell."

"So... what are you suggesting we do?"

Iona smiled. "I have something of an idea."

Roman's brow knit. "I don't like that look. Why do I get the feeling what you're proposing is really dangerous?"

"More dangerous than opening a portal to hell in the subway?" Holly asked.

"Don't you two worry your little heads about it," Iona said, taking another draw of her pipe. The smoke billowed from her mouth like some old wise dragon, and it almost looked like she was bringing the illusion of Elf-hame back for a moment. "Now run along," she said. "I need the space."

"Well hang on a second!" Roman said, but Iona swished her hand and the front door opened on the latch. She shoved them out, and the door closed behind her by itself. "Hang on!" He banged on the door. "Iona! What the fuck!"

"Come back in a few hours!" she said from behind the door.

"You could've given us a second!" Roman said. "I need my phone!" He turned to Holly exasperated. "Do you need anything?"

"Not in particular," she lifted up her own broken phone, screen shattered and dead.

The door opened for a second, and Roman's phone came flying out like something out of Mary Poppins. He tried to jam his foot in the door but missed.

"What the hell is she up to?" he asked, cocking his head to one side.

Holly shrugged. "Honestly, I don't know whether you noticed but I stopped asking questions yonks ago."

Roman turned, and huffed. "Coffee?"

"You buying?" Holly asked.

Roman patted the pockets of his cardigan. "Wallet!" He banged on the door again.

***

Holly sipped the jammy free coffee she'd tapped off Roman. "I'll get the next one," she said, making a mental note as Roman put down two plates — a fruit pastry and a thick caramel shortcake slice.

Roman smiled. "Cheers." They clinked their paper cups uselessly, the corrugated cardboard sleeves completely silent.

She hadn't sat outside in a long time. It was nice. Not too warm, not too cold. A church stood across the street from them and the road was paved with big elegant stone tiles. "I love it here."

"I can tell," Roman said. "Arabella was the same. A lot of her magic drew from the city too." He nibbled at a chocolate eclair.

"What on earth are you talking about, *drew* from the city?"

"Like what you did with the demon. You used your own connection to this city to release latent energy."

Holly's brow furrowed. Was that what she had been doing?

"Look," Roman said, buttoning up his cardigan against the wind. "Bloody hell, I wish she'd warned us, so I could've grabbed a jacket. Here's the first rule of magic."

He pointed down the street. She followed his gaze, past the casino,

94

the gilded shops, the white Victorian stone uniquely preserved by Glaswegian standards.

"What exactly am I looking at?"

"The statue."

At the end of the street, was the famous Duke of Wellington statue.

"I see him."

"He has a cone on his head." He did. A mighty orange traffic cone. He'd been wearing it as far back as Holly could remember. It was a bit of a landmark.

"Yeah, so?"

"How did it get there?" Roman asked.

"I don't know. Probably someone put it on his head on a night out."

"Well, yeah, originally. But it's been decades. You're telling me it *never* fell off? Never got blown off by the wind, or someone didn't get the joke and took it down? That whole time, it's been completely untouched?"

"Well, no."

"Exactly! It's magic!"

"What?"

"That's all magic is. A break in the laws of physics. The universe tends towards disorder, entropy. And yet, for years and years, the city of Glasgow arbitrarily decided the Duke of Wellington wears a traffic cone on his head."

"That's not magic though. Someone did that."

"Yeah. Many people, probably. Over a very long period of time. Magic. Because that's all magic is. Intention. We don't know why we do it. We certainly don't laugh at the joke anymore unless we're explaining it to tourists. But we make it real. We've all decided that the universe is wrong to knock the traffic cone off his head, so we put it back. Every time. Without even thinking about it. And that's magic. It's not just reading tarot cards and chanting in the dark. It's about deciding the order of the universe around you, and gently nudging it to be so."

"But by that definition, everything anyone does is magic."

"And isn't it?" Roman said, waving the paper coffee cup so hard the top almost popped off. "Humans, by their nature, affect change. Working together, we can affect change on an unprecedented scale. We defy chaos just by existing. Surely you must see how that's magical. That's why it's important to always be present in your decisions."

Holly took a sip of the bitter coffee. It clung, congealed, to her taste buds.

"I could go a cigarette," she said.

Roman laughed.

***

Holly's head was swimming with all the information she was trying to process, this new way of looking at the world. It was interesting, Arabella had been saying this stuff to her for years but she'd never actually engaged with it.

But wait. She *had*, hadn't she?

The demon's voice, unbidden in her mind — *"You have so much magic, but it's like you've forgotten it all!"*

As they walked down Candleriggs, its wide paved steps built for horse carriages, she could see it. She could see the hundreds of years of history sprawled out in front of her. The marketplaces, plying their trade. The music flowing from the City Halls. The restaurants, the people. And God, her own history. How many nights out had she spent walking up and down these streets, entwined between the gay bars that made Merchant City feel home to her. The cause and effect, the cascading actions of people. The tangle of time from days gone by, grasping, ever into an unseen future.

God, she was starting to *sound* like Arabella now.

But now, standing in the middle of the road, at the crossroads of Merchant Square, she thought she finally understood what Arabella had been talking about back on that night out. This concrete jungle, it was *hers*. It belonged to her, to them all collectively, and in claiming it they *made* it valuable. Like how we decided gold was more valuable than silver and built our entire world off of it.

"You've been quiet," Roman raised an eyebrow.

"Just taking it all in. A week ago, I was writing all of this off as fairy tale nonsense."

"You never believed in magic?"

Holly thought about it. "I don't know... I can't remember. As a wean I believed. Maybe even into my teens. All weans do, I reckon. But life has a way of stamping it out of you."

"Well, welcome home," Roman said, and he patted her on the shoulder.

She smiled. She *did* feel at home. There was a deep feeling of satisfaction that settled in her chest, that she'd not been aware she'd been missing.

"Where exactly are we walking?" Roman said.

Holly shrugged. "I don't know. I'm getting cigarettes. Iona will let us know when she's ready, right?"

"I suppose," Roman said. He looked concerned though.

"What exactly do you lot get up to?" Holly asked. "You know. When there's no demon to vanquish, or one of your friends hasn't disappeared into Fairy Land."

Roman smiled. "We run the Archive. It's the biggest catalogue of esoterica in Scotland. Iona's been collecting for a very long time."

"Interesting... How exactly do you pay rent with that?"

"We sell... stuff. Trinkets. Magical supplies. Plus, the usual, y'know. Incense. Crystals. Candles. Books."

"If you sell so many candles, I'm surprised you didn't set up on

Candleriggs."

Roman scoffed, a Cheshire cat grin spreading across his face. "That would be a nice bit of sympathetic magic, wouldn't it be?"

"Sympathetic?"

"Like calling to like. As above, so below. Everything is a reflection of everything else, and by drawing that connection you — Jesus Christ," Roman said, rolling his eyes. "I can tell every conversation with you is going to turn into a lecture. Just... soak it in. Make notes. Borrow some books. Ooh!" he snapped his fingers, rummaging in his cardigan pockets. He produced a small hardback notebook, red with embossed orange flames on it. "I was going to use this for recipes, but you can have it. Consider it your first Book of Shadows."

She took it. Ran her finger over the embossed pattern. "Is this a joke? Cos I'm ginger?"

"Happy coincidence," Roman said. "Though, that's a bit of sympathetic magic too."

"Does the Maestro have a pen?" she said, archly.

"One mo," he continued to rummage, pulling out a cheap biro. "There you go!"

She cracked open the spine of the wee notebook, and wrote down, *"Sympathetic magic"*. Then she put it in her pocket with her shattered phone, before returning the pen. "Right, one sec," she said, popping into the shops. Roman waited outside.

***

Roman banged on the door while Holly leaned on a column, finishing her cigarette. "Iona! Come on, what the hell is going on in there?"

"Trouble in paradise?"

A man poked his head out of the shop next door. He was a big guy, six foot something, thin as a rake, with curly brown hair and a goatee.

Roman jumped. "Oh. Hey Julian." He smiled. "No, not... well, actually yeah. We're having a bit of a crisis at the moment, and Iona's locked herself inside to cast some spell and won't let us in."

"Oh, well I'm sure she must have a good reason to," Julian said. He had a low, rumbling voice that spoke slowly, like clouds coming in overhead. She couldn't place the accent — somewhere down the Borders maybe? His voice was full of teeth too, like a broken fence. "Sharp as a tack, that one."

Roman rubbed his sinuses. "Sure, I guess."

"No sense in yous standing outside," Julian said. "Fancy a wee cuppa?" He nodded back into the shop. It was a music shop, it looked like. There were some electric guitars in the windows, a flute, a mandolin.

"You know?" Roman said. "That sounds nice."

He nodded and ducked back into the shop.

The inside smelled very strongly of patchouli, which didn't surprise Holly. It had a similar vibe to the Archive itself, with its eclectic antique furniture and relaxing atmosphere. There was no-one in it though, and the whole place could do with a good dusting. Julian fiddled with a teapot as Holly looked around.

"And who's the young lady?" he asked over his shoulder, as he reached for the teabags. He was even taller than she'd thought. "I've seen you coming in and out over the last few days. You got a problem in need of a magical solution?"

"I..." she said. "My flatmate, my friend, she's vanished."

"Sorry to hear that," he said. "Well, people disappear all the time. Hopefully she finds her way back to you."

"It's Arabella she's talking about," Roman interjected.

Julian turned round, looking at him. "Well, that is unusual."

"Why?"

"Well, she's always been a bit of a homebody, hasn't she?" Julian said. "Doesnae stray far fae the hearth. What reason would she have to suddenly wander off?"

"That's actually what we're trying to find out," Roman said.

"Well, if there's anything I can do," Julian said, as the electric switch on the kettle clicked. He poured tea into a teapot. "You ken where am are. I owe her a lot."

"Of course," Roman said. He sat down in an old armchair. "You know, Holly's turning into quite the young witch herself." He nodded to her.

"Oh?" Julian smiled. He had kind eyes, with heavy crows' feet from laughter. "Well, magic can come fae anywhere, ken. Hides in the cracks, dunnit."

"We were just talking about that, actually," Holly said. She smiled. "It's nice to meet you, Julian."

She reached out to shake his hand. The back of his hands were bushy with hair. He smiled and sat the teapot down on a little fold-out desk by the shop countertop. "Holly. You know, there are a lot of Hollies in my family."

"Oh really?" Holly said, sipping the tea. She couldn't tell if it was the type of tea she was allowed to ask for milk and sugar with, so she didn't.

"Hm. But then, you would in a family like mine. Holly is the plant that represents the winter."

"Oh, I hate the winter," she said. "Too cold."

Julian smiled. "I always think the same. But then the summer comes, and I'm sweltering."

"More of a spring man?"

Julian laughed. "No. Hayfever."

Holly cackled. "God, you're just not happy anywhere, are you?"

He beamed. "Well. I'm happy here." He drank the cup of tea, which seemed strangely small in his hands. She was having trouble focusing on him for some reason. "We have a lot to be thankful for in this world."

Holly nodded. There was something weird about this guy but

comforting. She wondered how Arabella had helped him but thought maybe it was too personal to ask. And there was something about the way he interacted with objects that didn't seem to make sense in her brain. But by the time she was thinking about it, she'd already moved on.

"God, how long is she gonna take?" Roman said, looking over Julian's shoulder as though he'd be able to see through the wall.

"A watched pot never boils, lad," Julian said, refilling his own mug then offering the pot round. Holly shook her head — in truth she'd barely sipped it. She wasn't sure this tea was for her.

"Apparently Arabella's in Elf-hame. But why?"

"Hm." Julian looked askance.

"You're from Elf-hame right?" Roman said. "What's there that she could want?"

Julian shrugged. "Whatever is here, I suppose. It's just another place. Folk gie it all this meaning because it's the Realm of the Fairies like, but, honestly, it's just like anywhere else. Politics, people, egos."

"Wait, you're *from* Elf-hame? There are *people* living in Elf-hame?"

Julian smirked. "She still husnae seen through it?"

"She's new," Roman grimaced. "It's a glamour, Holly. Look harder."

Holly tilted her head to one side, like she was trying to get a better angle. His hands cupping the mug looked too big for what she was seeing...

And then, as if a shimmer fell over him, the sunbeams through the window seemed to dance. He wasn't just tall — he was eight feet tall. His hair wasn't brown, it was pink and fuzzy all over his body, with a magenta puff coiffed on his head, his goatee, bursting from the top of his shirt. He had a tail. A big cow's tail that snaked behind him. His legs were goat's legs, and his grin, while carrying the same warmth, was toothy and jutted out. And Holly blinked as the first thought through her head wasn't shock, or fear. It was 'how did I not notice that?'

"You see what you expect to see," said the large pink faun. Julian's voice sounded exactly the same. And she could still see the glamour, on some level. It was like she was looking at two different pictures layered on top of each other, but now she couldn't unsee the true image underneath.

"Well, it's nice to meet you again Julian. The real you."

Julian smiled and raised his mug.

"You're picking this up quick, Holly," Roman smiled. "Honestly I'm starting to worry about my job..." He stared off into space behind them, before snapping his fingers. "Julian?"

"Mhm?"

"Do you still have that passageway that leads into the back of the Archive?"

"Unless there's been a cave-in I was completely unaware of. But it's locked on the other side."

"Not a problem," Roman said. "I can deal with that end."

Julian walked to a corner and opened a little trapdoor in the floor. "Well, I'm no gonna be able to fit in there, am I?" he said, scratching the back of his head. "Good luck to yous. Be sure and chap if you cannae get in and need to come back out this way."

"Oh, Julian Cherryblossom, you are a *saint*," Roman said, jumping up and giving him a massive hug.

"This better no get me in trouble with Miss Iona, hear?"

"Swear down," Roman said, raising two fingers like a boy scout.

"Good lad," he said. "Or, not lad. Lass?"

Roman smirked. "Your Majesty will do."

Julian guffawed. "Quite right." He turned to Holly. "Well, young lady, it was lovely to make your acquaintance."

"You too, Julian," Holly said, shaking his hand again as Roman lowered himself down the ladder. She turned to him. "Wait up!"

And as she clambered onto the ladder, she watched the large faun man wave and walk back over to his teapot, and she was struck by how she'd probably walked past this shop a million times in the past, walked past the Archive a million times, and the magic inside had been completely invisible to her.

chapter 16

The ladder went down a ways. As Holly reached the bottom, Roman stepped off into the dark and opened his palm. A small ball of light floated in his hand, casting dim light around them. The walls were stone brick, probably from when this entire street had first been built.

A few steps to the left, they came to another ladder. The tunnel went on and down. She wondered vaguely if every shop on the street had one of these tunnels, and if they did — if the owners knew about them.

When they reached the top of the ladder, Roman pulled out his keys and rattled with them. "Op!" he said, nearly dropping them.

"You couldn't have done this at the bottom of the ladder?"

"Och, wheesht," Roman said. With a loud thunk, he unlocked the trapdoor above their heads, and they climbed up into the archive's main room.

"Iona! What the hell!"

Iona, sitting meditating in a circle, jumped, eyes snapping open. "Roman? How did you get back in?"

"We've been banging on the door for ages!"

"Sorry, I was searching for Arabella. I can cover more ground by myself," Iona said. "But it's a fool's errand. I'm getting nowhere. Elfhame is just too *big*, it would take decades to search it with a hundred people."

"So, what, it's impossible?" Roman said.

"I didn't say that," Iona said, though it was clear she was thinking it.

Holly pondered it. "How could I find her by accident that one time, and not be able to find her now?"

Iona shrugged. "Coincidence?"

"You're the one always saying there's no such thing as coincidence," Roman said. "If there's a way to find her, we must be able to work backwards and come up with a spell."

"Yes, I suppose you're right," Iona said. "For all the heavens though I can't think what."

"Well, we're flatmates. And she's basically my best friend. Does that mean anything?"

"Yes, but not by itself."

Roman pointed. "They do both have Glasgow magic."

"Don't all of you have Glasgow magic?" Holly asked.

Iona strained her face to signify it was complicated. "Not... really. Though, you might be onto something. If the two of you are linked closer than even us, maybe you could... summon her. Pull her spirit here through the Astral Plane. At least long enough to find out where she is and come up with a plan."

"You mean a bit of... *sympathetic magic*?" Holly winked loudly at Roman, who laughed.

Iona furrowed her brow. "Well. It's good to know you're paying attention."

"Wait. If we're trying to connect using our bond specifically, y'know, sympathetically..." Holly said. "We should probably do it somewhere else."

***

Holly sat in their little poky living room, trying to ignore the fact that she could feel Iona and Roman floating about outside like spectres.

"Baby's first spell," she said to herself, laying out a framed photo of the two of them. She put in her earphones and blasted one of Arabella's old playlists. This room. They'd spent hundreds of hours in here, whiling the evenings away watching reality TV, moaning about lovers, eating and making merry. If there was anywhere Bella would be able to come through, it was here.

"Like to like, figure of eight /
My friend and I must communicate.
Hear my words, hear my riddle /
I send out a call, follow my signal."

The rhyming could do with a bit of work, she thought, as she tightened her fist around the scrunched piece of scrap paper she'd composed the spell on. But as she finished it, she felt the spell take root.

This room had seen a lot of magic, she realised. It had leaked into the walls like the smell of baking bread.

She closed her eyes, tight. "Come on, Bella. Come on..." she lifted a piece of twine that she'd pulled from Arabella's sewing kit, and suspended it with two fingers, letting one end fall to the ground.

With her eyes closed, she could feel the twine fall away. Like a fishing line into another dimension. There was no sound but the music blaring in her ears, but she was certain if she opened her eyes now, she would see the twine disappear into the floor like into a clear reflecting pool. She was so sure, she didn't even need to open her eyes to see that it had happened.

The earphones were suddenly filled with static. She turned her head, the sound was uncomfortable, but she didn't dare turn the volume down.

"Bella?" she asked, out loud. "Bella, are you there?"

The static faded away, a weak background noise, though the music didn't come back.

"Arabella, can you hear me?" she repeated.

"Holly? Holly is that you?"

Holly gasped. "Oh my God you're alive."

"How are you doing this? Is this you?"

"I guess I'm a witch now. Like you."

"Holly I am so sorry. I'm so sorry about your memories. I didn't want to do that to you, but I didn't have a choice. There's no time to explain—"

"We can deal with that later! How do we get you out of Elf-hame?"

"I'm stuck here. I'm trapped in the Queen's Chambers. If you go to my work and ask for Iona."

"Oh, I know Iona," Holly said. "And Roman. They're the only reason I'm talking to you right now."

"Oh, good! Okay!" Arabella said. *"Your wiped memories should've stopped you going there, that's really weird..."*

"Okay, so if I tell Iona, the Queen's Chambers."

"That's not all. There's no way the Archive will be able to break in here, much less get me out. But I have a plan."

"Which is?"

"I'm sending help. Someone who'll be able to lead you all through. Tell Iona to open the gate at the Queen Margaret Bridge, the old one. Midnight tonight. I should be ready by then."

"Wait, but Arabella—"

The sound was fading into static.

"Don't forget! Midnight to—"

She was gone. Holly opened her eyes. She was alone in the room again. "Iona! Roman!" she shouted, pulling the earphones off. "I got her!"

chapter 17

"Don't forget! Midnight tonight! You have to hurry!" The cosmic thread tying the two was starting to perish, turn to dust in her mind.

To hell with that, she had to do something.

Clearly Holly's memories were coming back. This was powerful magic she was casting. Whether it was because Arabella wasn't there to keep wiping her over and over, or whether this cell was dampening the spell in the first place... Either way, Holly was free. The shackles on her memory were being lifted.

Maybe it was fate. Maybe this was what was *always* meant to happen.

Closing her eyes, Arabella grabbed the cosmic thread in her hand, tried to pull up a big chunk of memory, anything. The more Holly remembered, the stronger she'd be. It had to be something recent. It had to remind her of who she was. What she'd learned. Her journey as a witch.

She gathered up the night of Roman's party, and cracked the thread like a skipping rope, sending it flying down.

***

The party had had all the usual suspects. The witch community are a hearty bunch but it's a small world. Every time someone new turns up they get passed around the room like a new baby, and Holly was clearly not taking well to it.

"Gin?" Bella asked, when they had finally made their way to the bar.

Holly huffed. "This is a lot, Bel. I'm feeling a bit overwhelmed."

She smiled, pouring generous swigs from an old bottle into two goblets that were shaped like swans. She topped it up with a plastic bottle of Schweppes Lemonade that looked incredibly out of place. "Och, you'll get used to it. They're good people."

"Yeah, I can see that. I'm just... so many bloody names! How am I meant to remember them all?"

"Don't worry, they'll remind you," Arabella passed one swan over. "To the next step on your new journey! Slàinte!"

"Slanj," Holly half-heartedly echoed, taking a sip.

If she could keep the wine flowing, Bella thought, Holly might actually have a good night and break the ice with the other witches in the city. It was all well and good for her to be studying under Bella as a sort of protégée, but she'd never break new ground if she didn't get any new input. She'd been trying to impart the benefits of coven and community, but she didn't know Holly was convinced — but then, Holly had always been a bit of a prickly old housecat in that way.

Bella swilled the swan, taking a big sniff of the citrus bite of the gin. "Good innit? Iona's been hanging on to that bottle for a while."

Holly smacked her lips, like she'd only just now thought to taste it. "Yeah, it is really good."

"God knows what she does with the stuff... Ah! There's the man of the hour!"

Roman approached, face already flushed with the drink, staggering and beaming like he'd won the lottery. "Bella, tonight is an absolute fucking beezer. Thank you so much for organising it. I'm having a fucking blast." He clapped her on the shoulder as he reached over to get the rum.

Arabella shrugged, with feigned humility. "It's just a Facebook event and a music playlist. I swear, it's like this lot are always gagging for a night out."

"You know what they say — weddings, funerals and Book of Shadows, am I right?" Roman nodded to Holly as he sloshed the rum in his glass a bit too hard. It ran down the side, overflowing onto the table. Roman didn't seem to care. His full focus was on Holly. "Do I know you?" His eyes flickered like he was consulting his brain's Rolodex.

"This is Holly, my flatmate!" Arabella put a hand on Holly's shoulder for support.

"Oh, the Holly?" he said to Arabella before fixing Holly with his crooked, toothy grin. "Lovely to meet you, hen! I've heard a lot about you! I've gotta say," he straightened Holly's tie. "I am loving the suit. Sharp as fuck, mate."

Holly laughed. "Nice to meet you. I take it you're Roman aye?"

"The one and only!" he stepped back, glass in hand, and did a twirl that made his purple skirt splay out. Realising the glass was wet with rum, he swapped hands to wipe his hand on his blue velvet shirt. "Look, I know you and Arabella have been like—" he clicked his teeth and pounded his heart with his fist. "Since day one, right?" He wrapped an arm around Holly's neck and pulled her away from Arabella conspiratorially. "But it's a fucking sin we've no' been introduced yet."

"I know man," Holly said, embracing the drunk gravitas of the conversation. "She's told me so much about you!"

"Well, I hope you don't mind me saying, I think of Bella as family."

He pointed to her. The rum was dangerously close to spilling everywhere, and the sweet smell of it floated around him like a perfume. "And that makes you my family too. Anything you need, right? Anything. You know where I am."

Holly had drunk just enough gin to take that to heart. "Thanks, Roman. That means a lot."

He clicked his teeth again. "There ye go." Then he looked up and spotted someone behind them. "Pete! What the fuck are you doing here man!" he shouted, piercing Holly's eardrum, and with a loud laugh, he was whisked away.

"Sorry, he's... intense," Arabella laughed. "He is right though, he's like my brother."

"You heard what he said?" Holly said.

"Holly, I think half of Merchant City heard him. The man has no volume control." Holly's glass wasn't empty, but Arabella refilled it anyway. It was that kind of night. Holly would learn — when you drink with witches, the merriment flows like water.

She wished she'd been able to show Holly this sooner. But then maybe she wouldn't have understood why Iona and Roman needed to be kept in the dark about Munro for the time being.

A lot of dancing followed, and Arabella had enjoyed so much mixing Holly with this part of her world — the weird feeling of crossover seeing her talk candidly in the corner with Aunty about queer spaces while Aunty regaled her with her tales of growing up in the thirties in a witch island commune of lesbians.

Arabella sometimes wondered how much of Aunty's stories actually happened. What details were romance, which were outright fiction. But that was the thing about drunk stories — in this state, everything is heightened. Everything is artifice, and everything is genuine.

She grinned, feeling the back of the chair she was sitting on the arm of as she just soaked in the energy of the room.

"*Alright?*" *Roman said, approaching, plopping himself down in the chair's seat. The night was starting to wind down, the frivolity had simmered into a few scattered deep conversations, like a pasta sauce thickening, rich and sweet.*

Arabella nodded. "Yeah. Alright." Her brain was soaking in gin, like a warm bath.

Holly plopped down on a comfy chair across the table, looking worn out. "I just saw someone change their hair colour with magic."

They looked at her like they were waiting for the interesting bit.

"You can change how you look with magic?" Holly said.

"Course you can!" Roman said. "Never leave the house without a wee glamour."

"How come you never mentioned it?" she canted her head, looking at Arabella as she reached to refill her wine glass from the bottle on the table.

Arabella grimaced as she tried to pluck the right words to explain. She was just over the line of too drunk for this conversation. "I used to use glamours all the time. Like, I used to leave the house looking like Sailor Moon, big doe eyes and a pointy chin and that. But it was kind of like using those Snapchat filters too much, it just warps your brain."

Holly looked confused.

Shit, Arabella had forgotten she was explaining this to the most offline person she'd ever met.

"Like, it normalised this unrealistic standard for me. And it meant when I looked at my face without it, it just made me feel worse. Like, three months after I was using glamours, my dysphoria was worse than it'd ever been in my life. Y'know?"

Roman nodded. "That makes sense. I can't believe we never talked about that before!"

Arabella shrugged. "Funny the important things that only go on between your ears."

Holly nodded. "Yeah..." She seemed to be lost in thought.

"Anyway, once I stopped using them, I realised I actually kind of like the way I look. Plus, I feel like I actually look like a woman now. I don't think, when I was that young, I really had an image in my head of what I should look like. So, I just drew this exaggerated picture of a woman and clung to it."

"I'm sorry you were going through that. I had no idea it was so hard for you."

Arabella waved her hand to bat away her concerns. "I'm alright. We're all on the long journey to self-love. And no-one can give you it. You have to take it. At swordpoint if you have to." She mimed holding up a sword.

"Man, I need to get you a sword for your birthday," Roman said.

Arabella beamed. "Oh God, don't, I'd end up murdering someone."

Holly shrugged. "They'd probably deserve it."

Roman cackled.

Arabella felt a squeeze on her shoulder and looked up to see Iona had settled down around them. A hand on a shoulder of both of her weans.

"How's it going, petals? You got enough to drink?" Her accent was stronger when she'd been drinking, and she looked flushed with joy.

Arabella nodded, waving her glass to show it still full.

"Good, good. Aw, it's nice to have everyone round," she looked over the room wistfully.

Arabella looked. It was looking like last call. Most of the people had filed out, and the remainders were in deep conspiratorial tones hunched over tables, talking about the past. A few tarot decks had made their way into people's hands and were being shuffled and spread.

Arabella gave Iona's hand a squeeze. Her hand was just as soft and delicate as it had always been. It had been Iona that had shown her makeup, back in the day. 'This is the first tool in a witch's sewing box, petal,' she'd said, wielding a fine-haired brush. 'The subtle arts. You can attract. You can terrify. You are your own canvas.'

"Love you, Iona," she said.

Iona tutted, her eyes looking a bit wibbly. "Love you too, dear."

Arabella wondered just where she'd be without this weird eclectic family of hers. And, for that moment, basking in the glow of them and Holly interacting for the first time, all her worlds seemed to come into a convergence. She closed her eyes and seared it into her memory.

***

The burning memory of that night sparked down the cosmic thread like the fuse on a stick of dynamite.

Arabella watched it vanish off into the ether. She had no idea if it would make it all the back to Glasgow, but she had to hope.

From behind her, a familiar deep, soft voice spoke. "Bella?"

She turned. "Munro!"

***

A smile broke over Arabella's face like the sun coming out as she saw Munro approach the bars again. "I was beginning to think you weren't coming back."

"Me?" Munro said. "Oh, even the grave couldn't keep me away. Ironically."

The two of them pressed their hands together, separated by the invisible shield between them.

"How much longer can we go on like this..." Munro said. "Arabella, we have to get you out of there."

"I have a plan. Or, I had a plan. It's complicated somewhat now. But it should be easier on your end," Arabella said. She lifted a stone from the floor, polished like fine brass and flattened to a disc. "If you skip this stone, it'll follow the path I laid out. It'll go home. My home."

"You want me to skip it across the Great Ocean?"

115

Arabella swallowed. "Would you do that for me? For us?"

"Oh, look at you with your big, sad eyes. You know I'd die for you, my love."

"Then do something harder," Arabella said. She took her hand away from the bars. "Live. Live for me."

Munro nodded. "How are you getting the stone out of your cell?"

Arabella walked as far away from the bars as she could, and then rolled it on its edge like a coin. It trailed along the floor on its own momentum, through the bars, and onto the floor.

"Take it," Arabella said. "Swim swiftly, angel."

Munro picked up the stone. "It's warm."

"It has my love," Arabella said. "All of it. So, it will move fast. You'll have to push to keep up."

Munro held the stone to her heart. "What do I do when I get there?"

"I have friends back home. I think together we might be able to break these bars."

"Okay. Okay. I understand," Munro nodded, hiding the stone under her cloak.

"I'll see you soon my love. They're expecting you at midnight."

"Who's they?"

"Holly. And the Archive."

Munro canted her head. "I thought... Holly was..."

chapter 18

There is a large bridge across Queen Margaret Drive, a hundred years old, constructed of a reddish marble immune to the elements. It crosses the Kelvin and connects the neighbourhood of North Kelvinside to the thoroughfare of Byres Road.

As far as records show, that bridge replaces two bridges, which were built out of competition by competing landowners, one the owner of a taxi company, the other the local bank.

Standing on the bridge we use today, you can still see the vestigial bumps of the old bridge, amputated in the 1970s when it was no longer safe. Pieces of rubble still litter the banks of the Kelvin, fallen from the old bridge now known as Walker's Bridge, at the foot of the most bizarre landmark in the West End of Glasgow — the descriptively named Sixty Steps.

Built wrapping around an enormous retaining wall, the staircase was designed specifically to entice visitors to take these steps down to the bridge below and hire a new-fangled taxicab pulled by horse to go about your fancy 19th Century business.

The design of the stairs and attached 60 foot retaining wall is credited to one Alexander "Greek" Thomson, a famous architect who appears to have never worked on another civil engineering project in his life. Like his namesake suggests, he was taken by Ancient Greek and Egyptian mythology, and the carvings into the large wall reveal these eccentricities. Arrow-slit windows like a castle. A large hearth seemingly for no reason. And most notably, the skeleton of an ornate door frame. The door does not open; there's no recess in the stonework, just an empty frame.

A few years after completing the wall, he died of poor health. The going suspicion is that the door was supposed to lead to the afterlife. And certainly, many young children speak of seeing the ghost of a second bridge in the shadow of the Queen Margaret Bridge, guarded by a spectral man with a jackal for a head...

***

"It's starting to get warmer out," Roman said, as he stood at the bottom of the Sixty Steps. They were waiting for Iona to reach the other side of the river embankment, where the bridge used to come out on the other side. Holly was smoking again. The dim orange glow of the cigarette was the only source of light this far from the main road. The street and the traffic somehow seemed further away than they ought to be, nestled as they were in the crook of the large retaining wall overlooking the river.

"Pretty soon it'll be spring," Holly said.

"God, what's the difference," Roman said. "This city is cold ten months out of the year, and it still rains the other two, I don't know how anyone puts up with it."

"Do you not like it here?"

Roman shrugged. "I do, I do. It's my home. But if you were to drop me on a beach in Corfu, I would definitely not be complaining."

Holly grinned. "Overrated, all that vitamin D."

"You would say that, look at you. You probably burn like a grilled tomato."

Iona's voice interjected in their heads. *If you're both quite done bickering, can we get started please?*

They looked across the river, to see Iona waving at them. Roman and Iona were each standing on a little bit of the path that jutted out, where the old bridge had once connected over the river. The water rushing beneath them was fast — it had rained recently.

"Okay," Roman said, gathering his breath, grounding himself on the concrete. "If Arabella's right, if we open the bridge right here, someone will come through. It's your job to catch them."

"Got it," Holly said, stamping her cigarette out and looking over the railing.

He raised a hand down the road, and there was a whisper on the air. Holly peeked round the corner — the empty door frame was glowing with blue energy.

He pulled his hand towards himself, and energy began to trail like plasma across the night. It reached his hands, and he threw it to Iona across the river. She caught it, like a rope, weighed it, and threw it back. And then the process would begin again. Building and building power in a dance.

Holly forgot that she was supposed to be paying attention until she jumped when the ghostly pale form of a wrought-iron fence was starting to shimmer into being between them.

"It's working..." she said.

"Stop talking, trying to concentrate," Roman said, breathing heavily in and out as they passed the energy back and forth like water.

Holly looked down-river, trying to see if there was anyone walking this way. If there was, what would they see?

And then she saw a hand reach out of the glowing door frame. Spectral and transparent, with bone and muscle showing through the skin. Then a second hand. A person was pulling themselves out...

"Uh, Roman?"

"Can't talk, busy," Roman said.

"Is he supposed to be here?" Holly said. The man had pulled himself out like the door frame was sticking to him, like he was dragging himself out of a pool of molten taffy. He escaped with a squelch, and then stood up straight. He was easily eight or nine feet tall, with the head of an ibis on an elongated neck. "I don't think he's supposed to be here."

Roman stole a glance over his shoulder. "Shit. I've no idea."

"What do you mean you've no idea?"

"I've never done this before!"

The ibis-headed man stumbled as he walked, arms dead at his sides as his legs carried him. Behind him, another spectral form was emerging from the portal.

"I don't know if we're supposed to greet him, or push him back in or what?" Holly said.

Roman looked over at Iona. "I'm trying to make out what she's shouting..."

Holly looked, tearing her eyes away from the jackal-headed man who was now stumbling after his ibis-headed companion.

She was throwing her head to one side, shouting loudly though they couldn't hear over the rushing of the river.

"I can't work out what she wants us to do. Why didn't she warn us about this?"

"I know what she's saying," Holly said, taking a shot in the dark. "We have to get rid of them."

"I can't take my hands away from the bridge!"

"I've got this," she said. Now that she was aware of the magic inside her, she was starting to get comfortable with it. She reached a hand up towards where the water flowed under the bridge, grasped, and twisted.

The river swells during the summer, and freezes in the winter, moving, always moving, she could feel it make its way down into the Clyde, into the oceans, and if she could direct its path—

The river, following her hand, ran up the bank like a tidal wave, wrapping around her, before hitting the ghosts, and washing them back into the river, pulling them away with the tide. "There! Easy peasy!" she clapped the dust from her hands.

Roman raised an eyebrow. "You're really getting the hang of this..." The bridge, still spectral, looked almost solid now. Glowing like moonlight, it looked like she could almost walk over it. Roman and Iona pulled their hands to their sides and heavy iron chains appeared in their hands, connecting across the bridge. They began to walk towards each other like some macabre funeral procession.

Holly followed behind them, trying not to look down. She could see through the bridge under her feet, see the water rushing past, the rocks which she'd be dashed against if she wasn't careful. Not sure if she could take the railing, her hands felt strangely unmoored by her side, as Roman and Iona met in the middle and tied the chains into a knot.

"Well done with the guardians," Iona said to Holly. "Though, I just hope they don't run into anyone before we hide the veil."

"All the more reason to do this quickly, right?" Holly said. "What do we do now?"

"Now..." Iona said, checking the little watch on the inside of her wrist. 11:57. "We wait."

chapter 19

Arabella twiddled her thumbs, feeling in the pit in of her stomach that there should be something she should be *doing* right now. But her whole world was this tiny cell, and Munro was hopefully on her way.

She looked around the room. The bare walls, the bars, the fog. She leafed through her little black pochette bag for what seemed like the hundredth time. Nothing. Chewing gum wrappers, discarded receipts, her little make-up bag. She didn't feel particularly glamorous right now.

She pulled it out and laid it out like a lock-picker's tools. And then she slapped herself on the head. "Duh! Arabella, you idiot, you're forgetting the basics!"

It was funny how sometimes you needed a reminder. She looked around for a reflective surface. Anything would do.

She settled on the biggest puddle in the room, interrupted every few moments by a pernicious drip falling from the ceiling.

It was like she'd always told Holly. Even before she'd told her it was magic.

"When you feel at your most shit, when you're at your lowest. That's when you need the little things." She said it out loud to herself because she needed to hear it, and there was no-one else around to tell her.

Magic.

The *subtle arts*.

You can plant the smallest of intentions, and let it grow and grow.

Nicnevin really should've had the guards search her bag better. She'd taken her wand, but that wasn't the most powerful thing in that bag.

She pushed her hair up in a hairband to keep it out of her face, and slowly, methodically, she took a face wipe to her chin, to her forehead, to her cheeks. To clear off the grime. Cleansing the space.

Eyeing her face for any spots she'd missed, she inspected her canvas.

This was probably not even the least appropriate place she'd done this, to be fair. She was getting flashbacks of her and Holly as young teenagers, sitting cross-legged in the out-of-order Morrisons' bathroom under the neon blue light with the stink of piss and the knackered cistern, locking the door behind them.

It had felt so... rebellious back then, so long ago. A statement. A flag in the ground, that no matter how many times other kids made her out to be abnormal, she'd wear that badge with honour. She would be anything before she would be like them.

Goddess, she hadn't thought about that in ages. Even Holly hadn't known she was trans then. She smirked to herself. Your teenage years always end up looking like you were living in a weird goldfish bowl.

Looking at the grime on the wipe and feeling the satisfaction of a clean face, she started her work.

First the moisturiser, then the primer. She could already feel the magic working. The little flutter in her heart that good energies were generating.

Foundation, concealer. The drip-drop of the water from the ceiling rippled her reflection so she had to stop every so often, but she was immersed. The grimness of her situation was fading into the background, there was only her face. Her easel.

It may have not been the face she'd wanted, but it was the one she was born with, and she'd grown to love it like a companion. And on a good day, when she was doing the work she loved to do, she would catch herself in the mirror, she'd feel this burst of euphoria to see the woman looking back at her. Confident, assured, the poise of an Athena, the wit of a Minerva, the grace of an Aphrodite.

And make-up wasn't the *reason* for it. But it was... intention. Just like when she'd been a teenager, it helped set the parameters of how people would interact with her. Part of an elaborate social dance. It was magic, in its purest sense.

A glamour she cast over the world to make them see the truth.

She applied the smokey eye she'd been trying out recently, viewing it from different angles, how it followed the outer edge of her eye, how it directed the gaze.

Just by walking through the world, I affect change.

She dipped her mascara pen and drew it up to fan her eyelashes.

My existence is a rebellion.

She contoured her nose, applied a lip gloss.

My gender, a refutation.

She applied a blue-tinged highlighter above her cheekbones, making them pop with a blue ethereal glow.

My femininity, a power that society couldn't take.

It was a mantra. She'd written it in a journal back in her youth. And she said it every so often, when things got low.

And the spell was complete. She eyed her handiwork in the puddle.

She wasn't sure what she expected to happen, but she certainly felt a lot better.

She looked up and jumped out of her skin.

Climbing through the window of the cell, were a number of little blue insect-like fairies. Shimmering gossamer wings, large curious eyes like obsidian gemstones. Their little hands and feet grasped the cobbled stone as they tentatively came in to have a look around.

"Hello there…" she said, leaning towards them among the rubble of her make-up and brushes. "I think I've heard of you lot…"

They looked at her, inquisitively cocking their heads like little puppies. She reached a finger out and one stepped onto it, beating its wings and causing blue dust to shimmer out.

"You are, you're little sidhe fairies," she said to it, raising it up to her nose. She suddenly realised she hadn't applied her setting spray yet, so she moved her finger back a bit, and it looked around the cell.

Sidhe fairies lived on the dust of magic. They must have been pretty hungry if they lived near this dampening field. Her spell must have drawn them in like moths to a flame.

They were all approaching her now, climbing onto her skirt, noses twitching as they sought out the magic.

"You know you're very cute, but I was hoping for some help. I don't know if you speak Human…"

The one on her finger looked at her like it was confused by the sounds she was making.

"Yeah, I figured not."

It smiled, a goofy little smile.

"Can you help me? I need to step outside, just for a second."

All over her body, they started to flap their little sapphire wings.

Arabella closed her eyes, and she was standing outside the cell watching this happen.

She clapped her hands together in thanks, looking in on the cell, where her body sat with its eyes closed, one finger still outstretched as a perch for one of the little butterfly fairies.

She was astral projecting. She'd managed to pierce the barrier.

"Oh, thank you little ones! I'll be right back!"

She probably didn't have long, but the astral form can fly like a bullet when it needs to.

***

Munro stalked the foggy hinterlands approaching the Great Ocean, aware that she was being watched. The trees here, gnarled and bowed and jaded to the drained earth they were rooted in. They had eyes and ears and were no doubt gossiping to one another. Word would get back.

Arabella's astral form floated above her. Astral projection was a simple trick for most witches, but as her body sat in that cell it was all she could do to hold on. The longer she was in captivity, the more she could push out. Like these trees, adapting to their environment. Pushing through the unfavourable dirt. She could feel the sidhe fairies' wings beating on her, giving her a lift.

Munro held the stone Arabella had given her in her palm, turned it over in her hand, squeezed it tight like a lover's promise. That was her anchor, with that beacon lighting the way she could stretch her soul this far. Munro wore Arabella's love like her selkie coat, it lit up like fire in the astral world.

Munro got close to the ground, ducking behind the bristly gorse. She sniffed the air, shifting her weight as she looked out. There was someone up ahead.

Arabella floated up and over, scouting out what Munro had seen. The gate to the Great Ocean was guarded, by one solitary man. A fairy of some description, he was tall and slim, with a staff of power sitting by his table. He wore the green military cut of the Boundary Folk. Basically, gate polis, from what Arabella understood. He sat playing a card game with himself. Arabella couldn't cast a spell — her body was miles away. Unless...

She approached a fallen rowan tree and reached out to touch one of its branches. Now *this* would be really pushing it.

Her hand passed straight through.

Nope. She wasn't taking no for an answer. She took a deep breath, aligning herself, and tried again.

In the cell, where her physical body sat, legs in a basket, the cold stone floor underneath her, she felt her hand close around the branch, and she was holding it. She ripped it from the tree — it twisted easy, the wood wasn't rotten, but it had lain for some time. It didn't come away even, the gnarled bark split in two at the end like a tuning fork. She held it close to her body — it was to be her sabre.

The guard looked up as he heard the twig snap, but there was nothing to see.

She raised the makeshift wand, feeling her magic channel through the actual stick in her hand into its astral form here, and waved it through the air.

"With all going on, with everything at stake,
It's probably a good time to take your lunch break."

He swayed on the spot, like his blood sugar suddenly dropped and made him a bit dizzy. He looked up, then down, then gasped.

Munro pounced. The guard flailed like a fish as Munro brought her arm up round his neck and held his windpipe closed with her bicep. He didn't flail long, as his eyes glazed over, and he passed out.

She dropped him to the ground like a sack of Maris Pipers. Arabella looked at the bruises already forming on his neck, feeling guilty. "Well, I suppose that's one way of doing it," she said.

Munro moved up to the door, looking for a keyhole, a door handle, something. But it was flush wood, emblazoned with a floral pattern across it in wrought-iron which had long since rusted. There was no opening in it, only enough to let the light through the bottom. "Now what..." she said to herself. She put her hands on the door, feeling around for some secret opening.

Arabella smiled, her heart swelling with fondness. It was like watching her dad try to get the VHS working. She raised a hand, swished the wand, and the door opened of its own accord.

Munro stepped back, then turned and looked over her shoulder. "Thanks, Bel," she said into the air.

"No worries, my love," Arabella grinned, even though she knew Munro couldn't hear her.

"Hey!" came a voice to the right of them. A group of guards, spotting Munro and the fallen other. "We've got a man down!" They started to charge.

Munro tensed, back arching like cat, her thick knuckles turning white as she clenched fists.

And then, Arabella put her hand on Munro's shoulder. "I've got this one."

Munro jumped and raised a hand to her shoulder where Arabella was touching her. She smiled.

Arabella stepped between Munro and the oncoming guards. They were going to have to do this, like everything, as a team.

"The sands of time, a constant flow,

Let the passing seconds slow."

She couldn't marionette them all at once, but she could do this at least.

An invisible bubble rippled around them, and suddenly their run slowed to a crawl.

Munro stood, looking around for Arabella.

"I'm here love, just go," Arabella said, but of course Munro couldn't hear her.

One of them finally reached the edge of the bubble and broke out into a sprint. She lifted the bubble, and threw it back down, stopping him again. She could feel her magic thinning, stretched so far and past the barrier. "Come on! Go!"

Munro looked through the open gate, into the Great Ocean beyond. "I'll get help," she said, resolutely, and charged through the gate.

Arabella threw up a hand, slamming it shut behind Munro. The guards charged as the spell dropped, passing right through Arabella like a ghost. They'd never catch Munro now.

Arabella stabbed the rowan branch into the ground, feeling her astral-self wanting to snap back like an elastic band. But she had one last thing to do.

Her on this side of the rift.

Holly on the other, back in Glasgow. Back at the source.

She forged a chain in her mind, an anchor that she slung to land back home, praying against hope it would carry Munro all the way back.

"Swim fast, my angel," she said, and the last of her magic spent, her eyes snapped open in the cell again.

chapter 20

12:05 am.

12:11 am.

12:17 am.

"This is starting to get dangerous," Iona said. "We're holding the veil between worlds open. Every minute invites danger onto our doorsteps."

"What else can we do but wait?" Roman said. He dropped a stick off the side of the bridge, and ran to the other side to see how quickly it came out.

"That's not what she's saying," Holly said, fixing Iona with a harsh stare. "She's saying, 'how long is it worth keeping this gate open, before we give up on Arabella'."

Iona pursed her lips. "I'm not saying that. I'm saying, if we wait much longer, we'll have more to worry about than those ghostly

Guardians. Maybe a better course of action would be to close the gate and try to con—"

The bridge shook, violently. For a brief split-second, it disappeared, and Holly felt her heart rise up her chest. They all flapped as they reached out to grab something. But then it reappeared as soon as it was gone. Holly clutched the banister, catching her breath.

"What was that?" she said.

Roman, who was already at the banister, pointed out. "That! It just came through the veil under the bridge!"

She looked. There was something flowing downstream. A large, dark shape, carried by the torrenting water. It looked like a body, Holly thought.

A mote of knowledge dropped into her head, as clear as day, like a single droplet of water falling into a clear lake.

"Shit, is that the danger you were warning us about?" Roman said.

Holly watched the shape disappearing down the river, and knew she had to act now. "No. That's who we're looking for."

"How do you know?"

"I have no idea. Come on." She wasn't sure what had come over her. It was like there was another version of Holly, another brain underneath her, and it was acting without consulting her. She grabbed the banister, lodged a foot on one of the iron-wrought fleur de lis of the balustrade, and prepared to vault herself off it. Despite the glowing spectral nature of the bridge, her foot held.

"Holly, wait! What the hell are you doing?" Roman said.

"No time, you get that gate closed again."

The River would catch her, she thought.

And she jumped.

***

The water twisted up like a mother's hand, encasing her lower body as

131

she started to rush down the river like the ibis and jackal spirits had before her. She could just about make out the shape, unconscious, rushing at high-speed like driftwood over the falls. She reached out a hand, trying to get the river to pick the body up, but she missed. Again, and again, but they were both moving so fast, it was hard to aim. Hurtling through the dark, past the old mill, they were coming to another bridge.

There was a tap on her shoulder, and she turned. Roman was floating on the back of a broomstick. "I said to wait!" he shouted over the rushing water.

"Let's get her!" Holly shouted.

"Her?" Roman said. "How do you know it's a her?"

"I don't know..." she said. Before she could think about it though, she had to turn, the river carrying her up sideways onto the underside leg of the bridge to stop her hitting it. Swinging an arm round, she righted herself and the two of them laid chase again.

Roman flew out past the unconscious body, up into the trees overhanging the river. He came to the next upcoming bridge crossing over the water and stood on the banister. He raised his hands, brandishing the broomstick into the air.

"Moon dragging tide, heed my song,
Down your tools, this is wrong!"

Holly felt Roman's spell take hold as it rushed up the water like a wave, causing the whole river to temporarily stop, become still, at the bridge. The unconscious body hit the stopped water with a crash, flying briefly up into the air, providing Holly a target. She swung her arms, and the river, frozen in time, flew up and lifted the two of them off onto the riverbank.

Holly rushed to her side as the river dropped them unceremoniously on the ground. She rolled the unconscious person over.

At first it looked like... a large seal. But then, the light shifted, like it had with Julian. It was a woman in a big fur animal-coat. Her skin was deathly pale, lips blue, dark hair matted to her face by river water. She was big. The biggest woman Holly had ever seen in real life. Six foot four? Five? With shoulders for carrying trees. For a brief second the disaster lesbian part of Holly's brain kicked out the logical part because all she could think about was how beautiful she was, rather than how she probably needed urgent medical help.

Roman landed next to them, throwing the broom to one side. "She's a selkie..." he said. "But that doesn't make any sense. You never see selkies this far south."

Another drop of water in the lake of her mind. More memories. "Her name is Munro."

"You've met her before?"

"I think so."

Roman tried taking a pulse. "I think she's still alive. Unless you know how to resuscitate a selkie, we need to get her back to Iona."

"I don't think we could carry her without hurting her further," Holly said.

Roman looked at her with a raised eyebrow. "Oh come on, babe. You *must* know this one."

He put his hands under Munro's back.

"Light as a feather, stiff as a board.
Light as a feather, stiff as a board.
Light as a feather, stiff as a board.
Light as a feather, stiff as a board..."

The spell began to take, and Munro floated into the air.

"Come on," he said. "You move ahead, make sure we aren't seen."

***

Sneaking back up the riverbank onto the footpath, Holly walked on ahead. Every person she walked past, she threw a glamour over. *How beautiful is this part of the city?* she said in their heads. *Isn't it gorgeous? Have a good look.* And lo and behold, they were too busy staring at the river to see Roman sneaking past with the floating selkie woman.

It was strange, how she'd just known how to do that. Or how she'd known how to make the river carry her rather than wash her away. Just how much had she learned with Arabella? Had she spent time with this selkie, in the forgotten past? She could hear her head thrumming, again pushing on the boarded-up doors in her mind.

Roman was watching her with a puzzled look. "Are you *sure* you've never cast magic before?"

"Honestly, I've got no idea," Holly said. "I thought not, but I'm starting to think everything's a lie."

Roman shrugged. "Well, you did just join a cult."

Holly looked at him.

"I'm kidding!" Roman said. "... Is what I would say. If I was in a cult."

Holly rolled her eyes. "Let's just focus on getting Munro back to Iona."

"So, you've met her before?"

"I think so. I think she..." Holly stopped. She strained, holding her head, trying to sort the fact from fiction. "I think she and Arabella were dating?" And then it all came together. "Oh my god."

"What? What is it?"

"Arabella's memory spell replaced her, with Podcast Boyfriend."

"Podcast Boyfriend?"

"Podcast Boyfriend wasn't even real!" Holly said. "I've been judging her for dating this rat-tash, part time DJ and really she was dating Miss Universe!"

"You okay? You look like you're gonna fall over."

"Now I know it wasn't Arabella who cast that memory spell. There's no way she'd delete hot girls out my head." She was half-kidding but trying to ignore that she could feel a simmering rage. Just how much of her life had been rewritten? And how much did Arabella know?

***

They could just about make out the bridge in the distance. "There she is!"

Iona was standing in the centre, wielding the two chains. There were zombies, climbing up either side of the bridge towards her. She was trying to undo the knot but before she could make any headway she'd have to turn her attention back to the approaching hordes.

She lifted her right hand, then her left, shooting two jets of air that sent three zombies hurtling off and down the river. Then she saw them. "There you are!" she said, furious. "Where the hell have you been?"

"Sorry!" Roman said, putting the broomstick under his legs and rushing off. The magic holding Munro aloft tried to follow him before Holly grabbed it like an invisible cat and pulled it towards herself. "Woah woah woah woah!" She lowered her hands to the ground and dispelled the magic, resting Munro on the ground gently. "We do not need you running away again." She knelt beside Munro and put her hands on her cold face.

"Part of the city, part of our home,
No one will see you, wherever they... roam?"

She was getting better at the rhyming couplets, but that one needed a bit of work. But she felt the spell take, and, with reasonable certainty Munro wouldn't be disturbed for the next couple of minutes, ran off after Roman to help.

***

Roman was flying in circles around the bridge, sending shockwave after shockwave of psychic energy to push back the zombies. Holly staggered up to Iona. "What do you need?"

"Cover me, while I close the gate!" Iona shouted.

"Got it," Holly said. She circled Iona, muttering incantations under her breath that didn't make much sense, but the intention was clear and that was what seemed to matter. "Back off, creeps."

Iona tugged on the spectral chain, trying to snap it apart.

"Power of the ancients, bring me your aid, we called on your magic to bridge through the planes.

That time is over, that game has been played, restore the seal, break down these chains."

The chains snapped, and began to burn away like ash and soot.

The bridge under them began to flicker.

"Run!" Iona shouted, and the two of them pushed past the disappearing zombies, trying to get to the edge.

They weren't going to make it. Holly could feel her feet starting to sink through the floor as it wasn't there any more...

A huge gust of wind at her back lifted her up and she landed on her arse back on terra firma.

She turned back just in time to see Iona drop, hand held up, and Roman on the broomstick to catch her.

"Bloody hell, never a dull moment," Holly said as they landed next to her.

"You should see us on board game night," Roman smiled.

Iona grabbed her face. "Well done tonight, petal. You were *magnificent.*"

Holly blushed. "Aw, I don't know about that."

"Where's...?" Iona looked around.

"Oh, Munro. She's down here." Holly led them to where she'd put her.

"A selkie..." Iona said. "That's unusual..."

"That's what I said," Roman said.

Iona examined her, before resting her hand on the back of her neck, cradling it. With her eyes closed she said, "I think her spirit just took a bit of a beating from the trip. If I share my energy…"

Munro gasped, eyes opening like she'd just had water splashed in her face. She clutched at Iona like a life raft. "I'm—! I'm—!"

"It's all right my dear, you made it," Iona said, gently. "Relax. It's a good thing we opened the gate for you, or you might have been dashed on the rocks of oblivion."

"Arabella!" Munro shouted. "I came for, Arabella!"

"We know, she sent word," Roman said. "What does she need us to do?"

Iona tutted at him. "Give her a minute to catch her breath, Roman!"

He cringed. "Sorry…"

"No! No!" Munro said, though it seemed like her limbs were still waking up. "There's not a moment to lose. I'm a representative of the Seelie Court, and she's going to be executed tomorrow!"

chapter 21

"The Seelie what?" Holly asked.

"Arabella?" Iona screwed her face up. "Are we talking about the same woman here? She widna say boo to a goose. What's she done that would get her put on death row?"

"She's angered Nicnevin," Munro said, gasping for breath. "We both have, and she's—"

"Hold on, girl," Iona said. "You're working yourself into a panic! Let's get you home first, get you cleaned up and some food in you, and then we'll see what we can do."

The street around them shimmered, the orange light of the streetlamps dissolving and shifting, and then they were standing in the warm light of the Archive.

Holly scoffed. "You could do that this whole time?"

"She saves it for special occasions," Roman said, rushing to the kettle as Iona lit the hob on the stove.

"I'm fine, honestly, just give me a second," Munro said. Her voice was softer than Holly expected, deep and smooth and shallow like a rocky riverbed. She tried to get up, but Holly put a hand on her shoulder.

"Hey, I don't know these people *that* well? But one thing I've noticed is that food is very much their love language, so just take it."

Munro turned, seeing her properly for the first time, and smiled with sharp white teeth.

"It's good to see you again, Holly."

"You... remember me?" Holly said.

"Of course," Munro said. "My mind wasn't wiped."

Holly opened her mouth, but the ten questions that popped into her head all tried to escape at once and jammed in her throat.

Iona flicked a finger down the hall and there was a sparkle and a flash of energy. "Bath's running. Your clothes'll clean and dry themselves while you're in there. By the time you get out, dinner will be on the table."

Holly scrunched up her nose. "It's not worth arguing with them, honest."

"Ok..." Munro said, clearly no energy left to fight. She got to her feet and padded down the hall like her entire body hurt.

Iona surreptitiously moved a finger across the air, and the door closed quietly with a click. "Holly, who is this woman? How is she involved?" she asked under her breath.

***

The three of them sat round the table as Iona lit her pipe.

"I don't really remember. It's like some of the memories still haven't come back. I get the feeling... she's *why* my memories were wiped in the first place."

"Arabella consorting with selkies," Iona's brow knit. "Oh dear, oh dear… I've known many a person to become enamoured by a selkie and it usually didn't end well."

"Can you blame her?" Roman said, whistling through his teeth. "My God, have you *seen* her?"

Holly laughed and tried to cover it.

"This isn't funny, you two," Iona looked serious. "Yes, they're all very beautiful. It's an evolutionary tactic."

"That's a bit… prejudiced, no?" Holly said. "She just nearly got herself killed to get here, presumably to rescue Arabella."

Iona shrugged. "You make a good point. If it's a con, it's a very long one."

Roman shrugged. "I refuse to believe someone that gorgeous could be evil."

"It's not a case of evil, Roman," Iona said. "It's much more complicated than that. The fairies have their own sense of right and wrong, their own axis by which they judge things. We keep to our separate worlds and try not to get under their feet, but you can very easily get yourself in a lifetime of suffering if you break one of their rules or taboos." Still she was looking at the door to the rest of the house, as though she was trying to work out if Munro was perched behind it listening to them. She took a deep drag of the long pipe and blew a plume of smoke up into the rafters.

"She was Podcast Boyfriend," Holly said.

"You keep saying that like it's supposed to make sense," Roman said.

"Everything else about my memory. It was wiped. Like there were pages missing from a book, and I would just skim over it. But Munro was specifically *changed*. For whatever reason, *someone* needed to keep her in the story but make me completely forget she was a selkie. She was replaced with some… lanky skinny hipster boy."

"Someone *you'd* pay no attention to," Roman said, as the kettle clicked. He got up and started to pour it into a teapot before getting a big tupperware of vegetable broth from the fridge and pouring it into a pot to heat up. "She must have been a big part of your lives."

"He was. He was at the flat *constantly*."

"Why would Arabella do this?" Iona said. "It makes no sense."

"I don't think it was Arabella. I think Arabella was just topping the spell up. I think I'd already started down the witch's path," Holly said. "And I just forgot it."

"Well, that answers why you picked it up so fast," Roman said. "But it just raises *more* questions. Wiping a witch's memory of magic is beyond any of us! There's no way we could be strong enough to get a spell like that to stick."

"But she did *definitely* wipe my memory in the street that time, I remember that clear as day," Holly said.

"Maybe someone else put a curse on you," Roman said.

"We would've seen if it was a curse though," Iona said. "When you first walked in that door, it would've lit up like a Yule Log on kindling."

"Then not a curse. Just a spell? A spell to bend memory?" Roman said.

"It would need to be a very powerful spell. From a more powerful witch than I know of. I think..." she paused, looking up and following the trail of smoke from her pipe as she went over it in her head. "I think we may all be in grave danger, and we don't even know it."

chapter 22

Munro padded back into the kitchen, rubbing her long hair with a towel, her thick and lustrous selkie fur skin carried in the crook of one arm. "You were right, I did need that."

"They always do," Iona said, stirring the pot of soup. "Especially when they complain about it."

Munro pulled up a chair which, with her sitting on it, suddenly looked cartoonishly small. She cleared her throat. "You lot definitely have a lot in common with Arabella."

"Where is she?" Holly asked.

"She's imprisoned by Nicnevin," Munro said. "For treason."

The look of bewilderment on Holly's face was clearly speaking volumes, because Iona filled in for Munro: "Nicnevin is the Mother Witch of the Seelie Court. The Patron Saint of the Buried at Sea. The so-called Queen of Elf-hame, if they can be said to have one."

"So... a big deal then," Holly gulped.

"A very big deal," Iona said.

Roman looked as lost as Holly did. "How on Earth did Arabella piss off this 'Queen of Elf-hame' personally? Am I missing something here?"

"I was..." Munro said, then stopped. She tensed, trying to force the words out. "I was forbidden to seek another. And then I fell in love."

"Why?" Iona said. "I don't understand. Selkies are encouraged to seek human partners."

"You have old information," Munro said. "But that aside, I personally was not allowed to. I'm... I was, in a previous life, one of Nicnevin's personal courtesans."

Iona's eyes were like saucers.

Roman sucked air through his teeth to fill the awkward silence.

"You were... oh that's not good. Oh, that's very not good," Iona got up from the table, pacing backwards and forwards across the room, smoking her pipe like a chimney.

"I'm sorry, I still don't understand," Holly said.

"Nicnevin is a very vengeful woman. Famously petty, with great avarice and power like no other witch has ever known," Iona said.

"I repeat:" Roman said, and then sucked air through his teeth again.

"We were in love," Munro said. "But she was immortal, and I was not. I was ready to die, old age would take me. But grief is a dangerous thing in the hands of a necromancer."

"She brought you back from the dead?" Roman said.

"We can do that?" Holly looked at them, unnerved.

"No," Iona said. "But Nicnevin can."

"But once she raised me from beyond the grave... it changes you. I didn't want to come back. And it drove a wedge between us. But she wouldn't let me go."

"I'm so sorry," Roman said.

"I was hers. I had always been hers, I loved her. But... then I was trapped."

"And then... you fell in love with Arabella?" Holly said.

A small smile broke through Munro's harsh face, a sunbeam cutting over a mountain. "She was... like no-one I'd ever met before. She was so kind. So passionate."

"Yep, that's our Bella..." Roman groaned, rubbing his face. "Fucking, Snow White, could make vinegar turn back into wine."

"What does that make you?" Holly said, shooting him a glare. "Dopey?"

Roman rolled his eyes. "Listen. When I fall in a mad love affair with the Evil Queen's henchman you can—"

"Roman," Iona hissed.

He shut up. "Sorry," he whispered.

"It went on for a few months. Almost a year, I guess. We would travel back and forth to each other, meet in secret. But we got caught," Munro said. She took a breath. "We got caught, and that was it. Death to us both. But I managed to appeal to Nicnevin's sensibilities. I still know her inside and out. I convinced her, it would be... *embarrassing*, if the rest of the Seelie Court were to find out what had happened. So instead, she wiped all thoughts of it from everyone else's head, and banished Arabella from returning to Elf-hame."

"So it was *Nicnevin* that wiped my memories," Holly said.

"To start with. It should've stuck, mostly. But Arabella had to keep topping it up. Your magic kept bursting out like—"

Standing on that street corner, the man's head embedded in the tree, the fingers of its roots digging through the concrete, finding the soil, finding the nutrients wherever they lay—

"Like I was trying to remember the whole time," Holly said. "Like there was some deeper truth that was being hidden from me."

"Basically. She covered the most slanderous aspects in people's heads directly, but it didn't stick to you."

"And you know this. Because... you never stopped going to see her." Holly was starting to feel the dots on her conspiracy wall connecting up. It all made sense now. "It was *your* voice I heard that day. It was *you* she was talking to on the other side of that circle. When she disappeared!"

"She couldn't enter Elf-hame anymore, but Nicnevin couldn't bind me. So, I would come here. And when I couldn't, those circles allowed us to talk," Munro said. "I'm sorry Holly. I did feel bad for you."

"We were friends? During those months," Holly said. It was all coming back to her now, flooding her brain. "Before my mind was wiped. We were *friends*." She clutched at her stomach, a deep unease in it.

"I didn't get to know you very well," Munro said. "But I felt bad for you, I'm sorry."

She had just started down her witch's path. Six months, maybe a bit more. It had felt like a secret club, learning the spells from Arabella, the mindset, the perspective. Tapping into the power of the city they both had called their home as long as they'd been alive. And then Arabella had brought home this hot selkie girlfriend, and it had felt like... Paradise. She had been living in a fantasy world. She'd been happy.

How long had they stayed like that? How long had that relationship lasted?

"It wasn't Arabella's fault," Munro said.

"I know," Holly said. She remembered that too. The affection. The two of them had been completely head-over-heels for each other. "I'm gonna wring this Nicnevin's throat."

"Get in line," Roman said. "Where is Bella now? How do we get her out?"

"She's in jail. She's got maybe a day before she's sentenced to death."

"How do we get her out?" Roman repeated.

"I don't know!" Munro panicked. "She said to come to you, that you would know what to do!"

"I do know what to do," Iona said. They turned to her. She wasn't pacing anymore. Stoic, smoking her pipe as she stared into space. The smoke rings circled her like rising incense.

"What do we do?" Holly said.

Iona spoke with a clipped assuredness. "We have to appeal the Seelie Court to overthrow the ruling of their own queen."

"That's not possible," Munro said. "Believe me when I tell you, the Seelie Court doesn't work like that. They're all basically gods, and they don't get in each other's way."

"I didn't say it was going to be easy," Iona said. "But that's the only way out I can see. We have to convince the fae to turn on each other."

chapter 23

It didn't take them long to pack a bag. Holly didn't have much to pack, and when she arrived back in the main room, the others were already waiting for her.

"Alright! Let's roll!" she said. "What are we doing? Magic circle? Bit of chantin'?"

"We're going for a walk," Iona said.

Holly looked confused. "You can... walk to Elf-hame?"

"If you're not paying attention," Munro said. "It was how Arabella used to come through, back when she was allowed. You can't get back out that way though."

"I see..." Holly said, though she wasn't sure she did.

They left the house, and Iona locked the door behind them. And then they started to walk.

Every so often, they would see a little street Holly had never noticed before, and they would walk down it only to realise that it hooked up to another street through an opening she'd never looked twice at. Capillaries between veins between arteries that she'd never travelled down despite thousands and thousands of circulations. At first, she thought maybe it was magic, but no — these streets had always been here. These side-streets. These little cul-de-sacs and back lanes and—

A bridge. They'd cut behind a housing scheme, through a little wooded path down the back, and ended up on the canal, in front of a bridge.

Holly seemed to be the only person surprised by this. There were whole extra dimensions to this city that she'd never even seen.

Iona was muttering something under her breath, some kind of incantation as she led them. Like a cross between a tour guide and a guided meditation.

They crossed under the bridge, up onto a side-street, on the other side of the river now.

"We travel the path, step by step, caution to the wind, whole-heartedly,

Climbing the branches of your secrets, to revel in your artistry."

Iona turned, one hundred and eighty degrees. They joined her, and Holly gasped, as her lungs filled with fog.

It wrapped around them like thick fingers, tendrils. Holly could still see the others, but nothing further. It was as though the world had simply vanished.

"Where are we?" she asked.

"Welcome to the Glasgow In-Between."

***

"What the hell is the Glasgow In-Between?" Roman asked.

"It's the very outermost region of Elf-hame, closest to the Glasgow Outwith. *Our* Glasgow," Iona said. "Now, be very careful. Think before you speak, don't offend any of the locals, in fact don't open your mouth if you can avoid it." She eased one of Roman's rucksack straps off so she could pull out the broomstick propped against his back.

Tapping it on the floor, the tip lit up like a halogen filament, projecting a little light around them for a few metres.

"You said you used to come here all the time," Iona said to Munro. "Would they recognise you?"

Munro shook her head. "I wasn't exactly advertising my presence. I was breaking the law at the time."

"Well, that's at least a bit of good news. Come on, let's see if we can find transport to Castle Nicnevin." And she led the way.

***

The Glasgow In-Between was... odd. She'd never seen a place like it. It was like walking into a funhouse mirror. The streets were wide dual-carriageways but all the houses were little and wooden, rotten and dilapidated from the outside. White fibre-optic cabling glowing with neon colours burst from the roofs, the seams between the huts, the pavement. The cabling almost looked like those little Christmas trees you'd put on a desk.

Holly tried to keep gawking to a minimum, but it was quite beautiful in how it caught her eye. She almost tripped over a large cable root which ran along the pavement.

They arrived at an old hut by the side of the road, with peeling green paint and a tile shingle roof. Outside was a little lamp post with a painted sign on the side that had seen better days: 'BUS STOP'.

Iona and Munro looked at the timetable, white painted calligraphy on a chalkboard propped by the door. It had the vibe of an old café. Still looking around, Holly locked eyes with a wee old lady who was sitting on a bench in the hut. She had a maroon cagoule over her woolly jumper and a big handbag clasped under one arm as she did her crossword puzzle

149

with a bookie's pen.

She looked up and smiled at Holly. She had kind eyes, squinting with her smile, and magnified slightly by the jam jar bifocals perched on her nose. "Alright hen? How's it goin'? Not seen your lot about here before."

Holly smiled, remembering what Iona said about not opening her mouth if she could help it. But saying nothing seemed even ruder. "Yeah, this is my first time here."

"Where yous from?"

Holly looked back to Iona, who nodded curtly before going back to the timetable. "Glasgow? Or... the Glasgow Outwith?"

She pulled a face of surprise. "Ooh, up the toon. I've got a mate lives up there, no' been myself though."

"It's nice here," Holly said.

"Aye, I've lived here about forty years. It's quite good, nae supermarket but you've got the wee shop there and the post office within walking distance. I'm just headed off to see my mate Shannon, her man's son's having a baby."

"Aw that's nice," Holly smiled. She got that vibe she got from a lot of older folk, that they'd been craving a bit of a blether.

"Where yous off to then? Yous look awfy dressed up, is it a wedding or something?" She looked around at them. She definitely wouldn't have called their clothes wedding-appropriate, but she supposed they probably might have looked a bit outlandish to an onlooker — Iona in her blue and black gown, Roman's poet shirt and layered maxi-skirt, and Holly with her Docs, her fingerless gloves, and her scarlet leather jacket.

"We're going to see an old friend of mine," Holly said, choosing her words carefully. "She used to live with me but she's out here now."

"Och that's nice int it," the wee old lady said, like she was barely paying attention. "It's so difficult to get oot and see people face to face nowadays, what with the phones and such. Op, there's my bus." She took her time getting up, putting her crossword book and her pen back in her handbag, standing up, checking with her hands that she had everything with her.

Holly had heard the bus coming, the familiar roaring of the diesel engine, but when she looked up, she gasped. The bus looked like a regular bus in most ways, but it was double the length of a normal bus, and instead of wheels a hundred human arms protruded. It walked along the road like a crawling toddler, or more accurately, a centipede.

Coming to a stop by the bus station, Holly could've sworn the hiss of the hydraulics sounded like a sigh. The arms lowered the chassis down like a palanquin being brought to rest.

There was a shimmer of magic to Holly's left, and the old lady turned into an enormous beetle-like creature. It wriggled its mandibles at her, and the old lady's voice came out: "See you later hen, hope you get through to see your pal alright."

Holly, trying not to react, attempted to nod. "Uh, yeah. Yeah, you too."

The enormous bug scuttled along the ground past them all and up through the door, pulling her OAP bus pass out from under her carapace. The bus driver, a man with one large eye instead of a face, nodded, and she scuttled down to find a seat.

"Are we getting on?" Holly said.

"No, ours is next," Iona said. None of them seemed to have thought any of this was strange. Holly saw the timetable now. It wasn't even in writing. Strange concentric ellipses that seemed to move even as Holly looked at them.

The bus driver pulled a lever. The old bus doors shut with a hiss, and the hands carried them off down the road.

"For a second there, I thought you were going to freak out and hurt her feelings," Roman said. "Good job, that would've been a terrible idea."

Holly swallowed to wet her mouth enough to talk. "What was she?"

Munro watched the bus disappear down the road. "She's an earry-wig. They love to gossip."

***

They were sitting around for just long enough that Holly was certain the bus just wasn't going to come, which was exactly when it came round the corner.

She'd expected this one to be towed by hands as well, but it wasn't. It didn't have anything at all. She watched it lumber down the road with amazement.

It would coil up like a concertina, and then fire itself down hundreds of feet at once. It hit the ground, putting a huge pothole in the tarmac, and then the hind quarters would start to retract, pulling it along the road like the power cord on a hoover.

"Is this ours?"

"Yes," Munro said.

"Not a lot of consistency with these buses, is there?" she asked.

Munro shrugged. "It's an old fleet. There's a lot of make do and mend."

Holly took a step back as the front half of the bus landed with a crash mere inches from them. The doors swung open, and Iona lifted the hems of her skirt and stepped up into the bus. "Four for up the castle please."

"That'll be an hour fifteen please," the driver said. He was a tiny man, three inches tall in his little bus driver uniform, and he was piloting a human-sized robot also in a bus driver uniform.

"Uh," Iona looked confused for a second, before Munro squeezed past her.

"I'll get it," she said. Iona was squished against the wall — it was quite a cramped space and Munro was massive.

She bit her finger so it drew blood, and casually, with not a hint of pain, squeezed it until red beads of fluid dropped into the fare collection machine. Holly noticed the machine was tinted brown by all the blood of everyone else that had done this.

Four tickets spat out and Munro took them with her other hand as she sucked the bleeding finger, and they all made their way up to the seats.

Holly sat down in the one of the back seats, determined to ask what the fuck that was all about later.

The ride was... unusual. There was a little bit of turbulence, though no more than a regular bus. But watching the view outside the window jolt forward through the air was giving her motion sickness.

She turned round and saw the potholes were disappearing on the road behind them. "Where do the potholes go?"

Roman in the seat behind her looked at her sarcastically. "Where do you think?"

Holly sat back down in her seat, trying to keep her eyes ahead for her stomach's sake.

Iona put a hand on her shoulder. "Won't be long, dear."

"I'm fine, don't worry," Holly said. She tried to focus on the huts going past, the strange fibre-optic cabling that made up the Glasgow In-Between.

chapter 24

She was right in that it didn't take long — fifteen minutes and they were standing up to leave again. Holly took a deep breath of fresh air, happy to be out of the concertina bus throwing them around like luggage.

Munro was walking ahead of them, stoic and eyes to the floor. Holly rushed to keep up as the others dragged behind.

"This is a bad idea," Munro said, probably more to herself than to Holly, but she answered anyway.

"Why? We need to get Arabella out, right?"

"This won't work. Honestly, if this was her plan, I could've tried to get her out myself."

"Why didn't you?"

Munro stopped in her tracks and looked down at her, eyes like smoking guns. "Because that was also a bad idea." She canted her head to one side, her dark hair tumbling off one shoulder over the seal skin. "I see you're as much of a terrier as ever."

Holly gulped. Munro's gaze was like a cold laser. It was like being looked at by a mountain range. Holly wasn't much used to people being bigger than her, but Munro seemed on another scale. She was an ancient fortress, built hundreds of years ago, who had outlived anyone who remembered what her original purpose was. She was a killing machine, a predator. Just looking at her, Holly could see Munro chasing down a fish bigger than Holly was in her seal skin, grabbing it with arm muscles like cabling, twisting and pinning it with her weight, biting through the salt water and gouging into it, blood pouring down her chin and her neck before she would shimmer and become seal-form in the foam, dragging it back to—

Oh, shit she hadn't said anything for like a full minute.

Munro coughed. "Are you having a moment, dear?" she said sarcastically.

"Uh, a bit," Holly said. "I do know you, don't I?"

Munro smiled smugly. "Your memories will come back. To be honest I don't know you that well, mostly just an acquaintance. That might be why it's taking so long."

"But it seems like you dated Arabella for months."

"Yeah, over a year. But a lot of that was, uh... long-distance." They were walking again, briskly. Holly had to power-walk to keep up with Munro's large strides.

"Right, the circle chat. Well, it beats FaceTime."

"Or jail time," Munro said. "I have to get her out of there."

"We will," Holly said.

"You sound very confident for someone with amnesia."

"I've seen how Iona and Roman do things. They're very touchy-feely but they're clever. And they don't half-do a job."

Munro grumbled. "I hope so. I feel so helpless."

Holly put a hand on Munro's arm, and hated herself for admiring the thick, soft bicep. Arabella and her big, beautiful girlfriend.

As if to remind herself of the fact that Munro was definitely off-limits, she asked, "How did you and Arabella meet?"

Munro smiled. It was the first time Holly had seen her smile. Her eyes glittered, like snow melting in the sunrise. "I found her on the beach, skipping stones... She'd wandered too far and somehow ended up in the Glasgow In-Between. I had never met anyone like her."

Holly felt a twinge of happiness cut through the petty jealousy. "She's very special."

"Oh, I know," Munro said. "And I know you know. My God, the way you interrogated me."

Holly cringed. "Yeah, that sounds like me."

"Your friendship was... jarring. I'd never had a friend who cared for me the way you cared for Bella. It warmed my heart."

"We've been through a lot together," Holly said. "Enough that I've almost forgiven her for wiping my memory. Almost."

Munro looked guiltily down. "It wasn't her that wiped your memory. Not to begin with. You can't argue with the Seelie Court, it's like trying to fight the tide. And at the time... you did agree to it." She cringed, knowing how hollow it sounded.

"I'd give the tide a run for its money."

Munro sighed, interrupted. "I'm trying to warn you before we go in here. Nicnevin is like no other person you will ever meet. Her will can bend the world around us, enough that she rewrote months of your life while in another dimension, without even thinking about it."

"I understand." She wasn't sure she did though, to be honest. If Nicnevin was so powerful, what exactly were they doing just walking up to her castle?

"I am sorry about what happened to your memories, whether it makes a blind bit of difference or not."

"It does," Holly said. Another lie, but it came easier off the tongue.

"It was part of her plea bargain. We could've rejected it, but the alternative was the death penalty. You were the deciding vote."

"I was there?"

Munro was silent. Clearly, she didn't want to talk about it anymore.

Holly looked over her shoulder at Iona, who was talking in hushed conspiratorial tones with Roman. She knew that look. A battle plan.

Munro looked ahead into the distance, as though she could see further through the fog than the rest of them. "We're approaching the castle soon. I don't know what your High Priestess plans to do, but surely it doesn't involve walking through the front door."

"I hope not," Holly said. "Though all of their amazing plans... not many of them seem to involve subtlety." She looked down at the ground. They were trailing a dripping reddish-brown.

She followed it back. Munro's thumb was still dripping blood from when she'd paid for their bus fare.

"Munro, you're still bleeding."

She looked down absently. "Oh." She lifted her hand to look at it, then put it in her mouth, into her cheek and sucked on it.

Holly blushed.

Munro snorted, smirking through her thumb. "Too fucking easy."

"You're doing that on purpose?"

"Holly, Holly, Holly..." she said, turning and walking ahead. "You forget, I've known you for a while." She spoke over her shoulder. "But I don't need to have known you that long to know you're a total mess."

Holly could feel her cheeks burning.

"What happened?" Roman said, as he and Iona started to catch up.

"Nothing!" she snapped back, sticking her hands in her pockets and trying to bury her head in her neck.

***

The castle looked exactly as Holly had imagined. Perched on the top of a very steep hill, it twisted in the wind like a wizard's tower. The fog, wrapped round them all like a thick blanket, kept its distance from the structure. The group stood at a black gate, of the kind you'd find in a field — except instead of timber, it was made of wrought-iron. The fence went on as far as Holly could see, which wasn't very far in the fog bank.

"There she blows," Munro said, glumly.

"The hearth of the Seelie Court..." Iona said. "God in heaven, I didn't think I'd ever see it with my own eyes."

"Let's just hope you get to see the outside again," Munro said. "Many don't."

"It is beautiful though," Roman said, taken aback for a moment by the spectacle.

"Come on, I'll take you to Arabella," Munro said. She reached over the fence and unlatched it, swinging it open for them.

There was a funny sensation as Holly passed the threshold. Something akin to sneaking out of bed at night as a child, the feeling you were somewhere you weren't supposed to be. This place didn't want her here.

***

The feeling didn't abate as they stalked through the grounds, keeping to the edge of the fence. The turrets of the castle seemed to follow them. A trick of perspective, one of those paintings where the eyes were always looking at you no matter where you were in the room.

"How many people live here?" Holly said, when the little path they were on started to snake into multiple directions.

"Oh," Munro looked puzzled. "No-one. At least I don't think so. There might be a groundskeeper. It's like our government."

"I see..." Holly said. "Then why hasn't Arabella just walked out? She's a witch. There are no guards?"

Munro shook her head. "You'll see."

They came to a greenhouse in the fog. Wooden slats and aged glass that was warped in places. Munro put her hand on the handle, took a deep breath, and plunged the door open.

A wall of hot, moist air escaped, and she led them inside.

Iona closed the door behind them as Munro trudged on. Holly had to stop to take it all in though. The inside didn't match the shabby exterior. Everything was made of stained glass, vines and plants and roses of blown glass in a million colours, choking around the passageway. As Munro got further away, she started to look like she was walking vertically like an M.C. Escher painting.

Iona grabbed Holly and Roman by the arms like a mother would. "Come on, we shouldn't separate." And she led them on after Munro.

Munro was counting steps, Holly realised as she got closer. '...seventy, one, two, three, four, five, six, seven, eight...' She spun on her heels at a crossroad and headed down the right fork.

Iona watched, enraptured.

Holly had a sinking feeling that if Munro lost count, they'd never get out of here.

It started to get darker, and darker, and Iona summoned a ball of light in her hand. The dim light played off the million intertwining shades of glass of the foliage around them, dappling like a kaleidoscope.

"God, don't you just wanna paint it?" Roman said, eyes sparkling in the lights. "I want to eat it."

"—A hundred and ninety." Munro's voice raised from a murmur to pointed speech. She put a finger up at her mouth. "Shh," she hissed.

"Sorry," Roman said.

They continued.

The light from Iona's orb was becoming less and less useful as the fog started to drift in around them. As visibility began to drop, Munro, still counting, reached out her hand.

They formed a chain, the four of them. Something about the hand-holding comforted Holly on an almost primeval level. Her hands safe, one held by Munro's large hand, and her other in Roman's delicate fingers.

"Jesus Christ hen," Roman whispered loudly. "When was the last time you moisturised?"

Holly snorted. "I think I got a free sample off Wizz Magazine when I was like, 14?"

"Aw man, I used to love their quizzes— ow!"

Iona had boxed him over the ear. "Quiet!"

Roman smarted. "That was sore!" They were stage whispering now.

"—Three hundred and nine, three hundred and ten..." Munro whispered. "Now we turn... left..."

She led them down another path. The fog was thick around them now. Holly couldn't see the end of Munro's arm as she led her further, further into the bowels of this bizarre place.

There was a click as they seemed to step on a tile on the ground, and Holly's heart rose up her throat—

"Wait one... two... three..." Munro said, as the ground seemed to turn them on the spot. She stepped off like a carousel, pulling the others with her in a chain. "Three hundred and fifty, three hundred and fifty-one... three — there!" she said, as the fog began to clear. She dropped Holly's hand and ran, coming to the little cell that Holly had seen in her vision.

"Bella!" she said, grabbing the bars. "Bella, are you okay?"

In the middle of the cell, hair dishevelled and eyelids heavy, was Arabella.

***

A half-awake smile crept across Arabella's face. "Oh, you're a sight for sore eyes."

"I brought your coven," Munro said. "I did what you asked."

"Thank you, Munro. I was beginning to think I was going to die in here."

"We're not gonna let that happen," Munro said.

Arabella looked, squinting to focus her eyes, and Holly froze.

"Holly..." she said, quietly. She started to well up. "Holly I'm so sorry. I'm so sorry about everything."

Holly stumbled towards the cell. "Arabella..."

Tears were pouring down her cheeks. "I didn't want this to happen to you, I felt so terrible, I couldn't—"

Holly put her hand up to the bars, and Arabella touched her hand through the invisible field holding Arabella in.

And then she remembered, *everything*.

chapter 25

It was New Year. New Year just gone. They were at a ceilidh.

The previous year was in the bin to be recycled, along with so much Christmas wrapping paper. And they were dancing. Because they were happy. Holding their hands together, singing, and dancing, stomping to the beat, and just enough people knew the moves that everyone could join in.

Arabella had her long hair up in a bun and wore a black shirt and tartan skirt. She wouldn't have looked out of place among the band. Holly's cheeks hurt from laughing so hard all night. The two of them were standing at the bar, waiting to be served — though really it was just an excuse to catch their breath. The dancing was burning the alcohol out of their systems as fast as they could drink it.

"I have something to tell you," Arabella said. "And uh, not much time to tell you in."

Holly screwed up her face. "What's up?"

"I have a first date tonight?" Arabella said. "It's pretty serious, I've been talking to her for a couple months."

"Oh shit!" Holly grinned. "Congrats. How did you keep that quiet?"

"She's... the strong silent type," Arabella said. Holly was full of questions as Arabella turned away to order them the customary double-vodka-soda-limes they'd been tanning all evening. "She's a selkie."

Holly's eyes widened. "I didn't think that was allowed!"

Arabella looked more chipper than Holly had ever seen her. "It's not!" Like a little kid who had found where the Christmas presents were kept.

"Goody-two-shoes Arabella Morrow, courting a selkie. You not worried she's gonna compel you into the ocean or something?"

"Oh God, Holly, I'd go if she asked me. She's just amazing." She rested her hand on Holly's shoulder and smiled.

Holly smiled wistfully, a buoyant warmness in her heart that mixed well with her tipsiness. "I'm so happy for you, Bella!"

"Thanks," she smiled. "She's actually due here any minute." She took the two glasses from the bartender and passed one to Holly. They locked drinking arms around one another, like a primal bonding spell.

"Slàinte!" they shouted, and drained them. The sharp taste of the vodka made Holly's brain tingle pleasantly.

"Happy New Year, Bella," she smiled. Her first Hogmanay as a witch. It felt auspicious. New beginnings.

Arabella gasped. "There she is! She's here!" she checked her reflection and her hair in one of the beer-taps futilely.

Holly spun to look at the door. A very tall glass of water with piercing grey eyes and a prim blue tuxedo was standing in the doorway, looking incredibly uncomfortable and awkward.

Holly gasped. "Oh my God Bella she's gorgeous how the fuck did you manage that!" She elbowed her friend in the ribs repeatedly. "Go! Fuckin' go! Fire in!"

Arabella cackled, swatting at her as she doubled over laughing.

They'd all spent the night dancing until their limbs ached. They thought about the past, and all the people they'd lost. For that moment, they were all together. They all got very drunk and celebrated themselves.

Well done, everyone. Another year down. Here's to the next one.

And she had forgotten all of that.

***

"I'd been a witch for..." Holly realised. "I lost almost a full year of my life."

In comparison to the girl in the tartan skirt, Bella looked haggard and wan from her time in the cell. Like what people said witches looked like in story books.

"Yes," Arabella said. "You were a quick student, Holly. And I'm sorry I took that away for my own gain."

"Arabella..." Holly said, welling up at the sight of her friend so upset. "You're so important to me. Your life was on the line. I don't blame you."

Arabella wiped her eyes on her sleeve. "Well, you wouldn't, would you. Bloody martyr."

They both laughed through burbling tears.

"I'm still sorry, it was so horrible. And it was horrible watching you, you have no idea. To re-wipe you every time you started to remember."

"Well, I remember now," Holly smiled. "And we're gonna get you out of there." She turned, and suddenly realised she'd been greetin' like a wee baby in front of everyone.

Roman was looking at the wall like there was a stone on there that was completely fascinating. Iona smiled at Arabella. "Good to see you, petal."

"Oh my god, it's so good to see you two."

"How are we getting you out of there?" Roman asked.

"How indeed..." came a whispering voice from down the corridor.

Holly felt a chill come over her bones.

***

The three witches in the hallway stumbled, each trying to step between the assailant and the others, a clumsy show of protection for one another that was each tripped up by the others doing it for them.

"What are you doing in here?" Nicnevin said, squeezing herself through the door frame one shoulder at a time. She stood to her full height, and Holly felt her knees start to tremble.

She certainly looked like a queen of the witches, she thought to herself, as Nicnevin straightened up as much as she could and pushed lustrous jet-black hair out of her eyes with long, shining black nails.

"This is the woman you pissed off?" she said under her breath looking at Munro and Arabella.

Iona cleared her throat, taking a tentative step towards the Mother Witch. "Mistress Nicnevin, it is a pleasure to make your acquaintance, even under these circumstances." Her voice was clipped — even moreso than normal, the islander burr on full show. Her throat sounded dry, and she swallowed.

Nicnevin smiled, and there was a glint in her eyes that stood out against her teal blue skin. "You know the old ways, it seems. Wise beyond your years..." She pursed her lips like she was trying to make something out on the horizon. "Iona NicMhànais."

Iona smiled. "That's my maiden name," she corrected. "I became Iona Howell. Though I suppose I don't have any claim to that name anymore either."

"All of you are on the path it seems..." Nicnevin said, and she took a large step further into the hallway towards them. Iona flinched as the Mother Witch's gaze fell over them all in turn like a spotlight. She squinted at them, trying to pluck their names from the Weave. "Roman Buchanan. Holly Winter." Then she scoffed, looking almost *offended* at

Holly. "You."

"Me," Holly said, swallowing so her dry throat didn't crack.

"I dealt with you. What are you doing here? How did you find your way back onto the path?"

"I remembered what you took," Holly said. "How could you do that to me?"

Nicnevin smiled. "Oh, you poor little mortal. But the truth is, it was very easy. Your minds are all so tiny, and yours in particular has a laser focus. It's an easy thing to direct it elsewhere."

Holly heard herself breathing heavily, balled her hands into fists. She was shaking. "How could you be so cruel?"

"Oh, child. The memory of a mortal is worth less than the air they breathe. You all forget almost everything you ever learn. You are pliable, and chaotic."

Iona turned to Holly, fear in her eyes. "Remember what I told you..."

But Holly could feel the blood pounding in her ears. They meant *nothing* to her, and she'd all but ruined their lives.

"Let my friend go!" Holly shouted, jabbing a finger at the jail cell. "She hasn't done anything wrong!"

"Hasn't done anything wrong?" Nicnevin scoffed. "She stole from me. She humiliated me, in front of all my peers. I will still be dealing with the dishonour she put on my name when you are all dust."

"Get to fuck!" Holly shouted. "She doesn't owe you shit!"

Iona was breathing heavily. "Holly..."

The passive, almost absent interest in Nicnevin's face twisted, at once, into rage. Thunder clapped outside, the fog began to encroach through the windows, as the hallway seemed to darken, and lengthen, Nicnevin's anger becoming one with the shadows. "Wordy little whelp. Your insults are large, but your power is small..."

"I have more power than you think," Holly said. She could feel her anger around herself. It hung on her shoulders, wrapped round her like a heavy cloak, and she knew how to wear it now.

She had all the power of her Glasgow magic, and this close to Arabella? Her best friend? Her teacher? Another Glasgow witch? She could do anything.

She charged.

"Holly!" Iona screeched. Roman made a lunge to grab for her, but he was too lanky, and she swerved under his arm.

She might not have been able to reach Nicnevin, were she not stooping with the low ceiling. But she remembered exactly what to do. She'd seen Arabella do it. She could feel it in her soul.

She grabbed the witch by the lapel, reared her head back, and planted the Glasgow Curse on her nose.

For a moment, stars shone in both of their eyes as there was a burst of verdant green magic through the room.

Nicnevin staggered back, as Holly drifted like a feather to the ground.

Iona rushed forward and grabbed Holly by the arms, trying to pull her back, back to safety...

"Holly what have you done?" Roman was pale, trembling.

Holly grinned, feeling pleased with herself. Then she turned and saw Arabella staring at her in shock as well. Her smile faltered.

She turned to Nicnevin, expecting to see the tree starting to grow, for her to be hitting the ground.

But instead, she was standing back up, and all that was dripping from her nose was blood.

Nicnevin laughed. A little at first, and then large cackles. "Really?"

Iona held a vice grip on Holly's arms like she was worried Holly was going to get dragged away any moment.

Nicnevin wiped the single droplet of blood from her nose and looked at it, like it was someone else's. "Really?" she asked again. "*People make Glasgow?"* She cackled again. "And what are other cities made out of? What makes Paris? *Croissants?"*

Holly staggered back, bumbling with her words, as Nicnevin advanced on them like a jungle cat.

"Understand me well, Holly of the Winter. This is a spell you've all cast on yourselves. A magic you all opted into. A story you self-perpetuate." She was furious now, hands shaking, nails clawing the air. "You polish the brightness to a mirror shine while ignoring that the silver was made off the backs of slaves. You use the idea of Empire to launder your sins, to sanitise yourselves. Victimise yourselves. Glasgow made the tobacco money. Glasgow sold human beings as property."

She snorted, smoke escaping her nose like a dragon. She looked to Iona. "It even turns inwards." She looked back at Holly. "Just who do you think carried out the Clearances? You turned your back on your countrymen, you pillaged their communities. And now you want to act like you're all one big happy family, *when it suits you*. And you tut-tut and say, 'that's not us' when sectarians destroy George Square twice a year."

Holly took another step back, but she'd run out of room to retreat. She was backed up against the wall. With a swipe of Nicnevin's hand, the others between the two of them were pinned to the wall by a magical force.

"No freedom until we're all free, isn't that what you think it's all about? Well, it wasn't true then, and it isn't true now. Is it? You spent thirteen years in school, thinking other gay people didn't even exist. And just how long did Arabella have to sit on that waiting list? Watching her body change against her will, while waiting for life-saving medicine that the doctors were giving out to cis people for menopause and baldness."

The smoke billowing from Nicnevin's nose and mouth were starting to entwine the two of them now. Nicnevin approached, raising a hand—

But it stuck on something. She turned.

Arabella, one arm stretched out of the cell, was holding onto Nicnevin's sleeve for dear life.

"Eh, Nicnevin," she said, tears of rage in her eyes. Her clipped West End affectation was dulled by emotion. "You literally have me locked in a cage right now. So maybe don't talk about my rights?"

"Oh, your moment is coming, Ms. Morrow," Nicnevin said. "Don't worry about that." She snapped her fingers, and Arabella was thrown across the room.

Unperturbed, Nicnevin turned towards Holly. This close, her face felt almost as big as Holly was. Like some sea monster that could swallow entire ships without thinking about it. Her magic held Holly in place on a cellular level. She couldn't even breathe. She was nothing before this power.

"Little insect prattling on,
You shall not live to see the dawn.
With all the power in my spell,
I banish thee to hell."

The smoke rose into Holly's lungs, she took one deep gasp, and then the world faded to black.

chapter 26

Arabella sat on the cold pew, taking deep shuddering breaths. This had been the very place she'd been trying not to end up, and now she'd made things worse and implicated her friends.

The front row of the pew held Iona, Roman, then her. The justices promenaded down the central aisle, solemn like a funeral procession. There were three of them, all ten feet tall.

A man with a long velvet cape and flowing red hair, butterflies in a hundred colours floating around his head and alighting his cheekbones, with an aurora-like trail behind him.

A woman dressed head to toe in petticoats of a deep red with a black chiffon gown hanging over. Black horns studded with little rubies and diamonds protruded from her forehead and looped backwards, a delicate earring chain cuff connected between her left horn and one of her long, pointed fairy ears. A long cow tail poked out the back of her dress and swished as she walked.

And behind her, Nicnevin. Her teal skin glimmering in the low light of the room, her long raven hair tied up to accentuate her neck, and her dress trailing behind her like the wake of a mighty boat. She locked eyes with Arabella almost absently as they proceeded to their place at the front of the courtroom, and it sent a cold chill through Arabella.

Munro walked behind them a good few feet. Her hair was matted, her steps shuffling, her head low to the ground like a beaten dog. Arabella tried to get her attention as she walked past, but she could smell the magic pouring off of her. There was a powerful mind control hex branded on her. Everyone else in the room may as well not have been here.

"Oh God, what have I done..." she said to herself.

"Arabella," Iona whispered, leaning over Roman and shaking her arm to get her attention. "How much do you know about how these trials work?"

"Only what Munro's told me. You represent yourself. You need to convince two out of three justices that either you're innocent, or that you don't deserve to be punished."

Iona sat up in her chair and straightened her back. "So, they're judge, jury and executioner..."

"Nicnevin's on the jury? That doesn't seem very fair," Roman said.

"I think the idea is that if you're innocent it doesn't matter who's on the jury. Plus, if—" Arabella started, but before she could explain further, Nicnevin and the others had taken their seats at the table at the front, and Nicnevin clinked a spoon off a crystal goblet.

The rabble behind them quieted to a dull roar and the three of them sat very straight.

"Court is now in session," Nicnevin said, projecting her voice so, even in the rafters, people could hear. A number of ornamental candles down the sides of the pews lit, casting a dull glow which pushed back the moonlight.

It felt more like a church than a courtroom, Arabella thought. The candles, the pews, the altar they were all sitting behind.

"Three human witches stand before us today, accused of conspiracy, of treason, and of stolen property," Nicnevin said. "Today we will discover if the court finds them Seelie or Unseelie."

Arabella could feel the boke rising in her and swallowed. They were doomed.

"The court calls Iona Howell, née NicMhànais, to triage."

Iona stiffened next to them. Then, she stood, brushed down her front, took a deep breath, summoned her broomstick out of thin air, and approached the altar.

Her boots clacked on the stone floor, and she stood, head tall, shoulders back. "Lords and Ladies of the Court," she said. "Thank you for the honour of allowing me to present my case today." She bowed, deeply.

Nicnevin rolled her eyes. The man with the butterflies on his face looked flattered.

"Today I'd like to make the case to you that both I and my friends are completely innocent of all crimes that we have been accused of. There's no basis for any of this, we weren't even aware of any of this. I will do so using—"

The woman with the horns yawned pointedly. "God, I'm bored," she said, cutting Iona off.

"I'm sorry?" Iona said.

"This is boring, you're boring me," she said. "Is anyone else bored?"

A twinge of fear ran up Arabella's back. She knew what was coming. "Oh God, Iona, what are you doing?"

Roman screwed up his face.

"I... sorry, I'm afraid I don't understand," Iona said.

The woman raised her hand, looking to the other judges. "Guilty?"

The man with the butterflies shrugged. "Guilty."

"Guilty," Nicnevin said, a smile spreading across her face.

Iona, jaw moving up and down like a fish, trying to process what had just happened, said nothing.

"Iona Howell, I sentence your memory to my collection," Nicnevin said. "The world will forget you henceforth."

She snapped her fingers, and Iona turned to dust before them. Her broomstick clattered to the ground.

Roman grabbed Arabella's hand next to him. "What... what was that?"

"She didn't get it," Arabella said, under her breath. "Roman, it's not really a trial, it's a pageant. It's reality TV. They're tricksters. You have to put on a show, you have to make them *like* you enough to decide you're innocent or decide they don't want to punish you."

Roman paled, then smiled weakly. "Oh. Why didn't you say so?"

Nicnevin tapped her spoon off her goblet again before taking a large swig of whatever amber liquid was inside. "The court calls Roman Buchanan to triage."

Roman stood up, and foofed his hair.

"You can do this, Roman," Arabella said.

"Honey, the trauma of the last five minutes aside," he threw his head back over his shoulder to look at her. "I think I was made for this."

chapter 27

Holly's consciousness swam. It felt similar to when she'd zipped up the World Tree into the varying dimensions, but... deeper. Like she was underwater. Drowning. Pulled here and there by currents that had been moving since before she was born.

But in the dark, she could hear voices. A chorus. Off in the distance.

"Skip a page in the cosmic tome,
Send her away, send her home.
Skip a page in the cosmic tome,
Send her away, send her home.
Skip a..."

It continued, a chant of power. Roman and Iona and... Arabella.

"What are you doing?" she asked, but though she could feel her throat make the sound, she heard nothing. As though she were in space.

She was going to Hell... she realised. There was nothing she could do, there was—

She gasped, the wind knocked out of her as the light came flooding back in. She landed on something soft.

She sat up, coughing and spluttering, her eyes still adjusting. She reached her hands out. A ratty couch the colour of green curry. Moth-eaten old curtains on bare wooden floorboards.

She was home.

"But how?" she asked, looking around. "How did I get here?"

She stood, and waved her hands in the air, trying to pull back the celestial thread that had carried her back. And for a second, she saw it. The room where Nicnevin had banished her to Hell.

Her coven... chanting under their breath. Unable to stop the spell... but able to twist it, ever so slightly, so instead of where Nicnevin intended, it had brought her here.

They'd saved her life, she thought. She had to...

But as soon as she'd seen the echo of what had happened, it had started to fade. Like the last ember of a candle before it ran out of wax, it flashed, and was gone, leaving only the burnt thread of the wick.

She fell to her knees. "But wait... I need to be there... I need to..."

And she burst into tears.

***

Stepping out the front door in yesterday's clothes, she sucked in air and clenched her teeth as the cold bit through her jacket. It was pitch black. What time was it? She checked her phone — still broken.

With no way to know, she walked down the street anyway. No one was around, the streets were quiet as a Tory's funeral. It took on an almost liminal nature. Just her and the sandstone buildings, holding back the wilderness. Alone. The only one who was safe.

She wiped the tears from her eyes. There was no point greeting. They were still back there, and they needed her help.

Wandering down Argyle Street in the dark, she was amazed to find even the main road didn't have anyone on it. She was beginning to think she wasn't back home at all, but in some shadowy parallel dimension, slightly off-kilter from the real one.

But then she got to the end of the street, up Trongate, and came to the clock tower at the Tron Theatre. A quarter to five.

4:45 am, no wonder no-one was about.

Pulling her jacket around her tighter, willing the sun to rise, she turned right and headed down towards the Archive.

***

She didn't know what she expected. There was, obviously, no one in. She stood outside it, looking at the corrugated iron shutters over the door, and, on autopilot, pulled her cigs from her pocket and lit one.

The smoke didn't calm her nerves though and looking at the Archive all cold and empty just reminded her that if she didn't do something, and fast, that shutter would never come up.

A dim lamplight shone out of Julian's shop. It was still too dark to make out any details of the interior, but someone was wandering about inside.

She chapped the window.

There was a noise inside of faffing about and then the door popped open. Julian stuck his big fluffy head out the door, looking around the plaza. "Something the matter, Holly? You're up awfy early."

She opened her mouth to try and summarise, but then a few seconds went by where no sound came out and she just huffed air out exasperatedly.

Julian furrowed his bushy magenta eyebrows. "That bad, eh?" He shrugged. "They'll no' be up yet. 'Mon in and I'll make you a wee coffee." He smiled, the corners of his eyes crinkling. "I got it in after making yous drink my stuff."

Holly stubbed the butt of her cigarette out on a bin. "I don't know if you can help me."

"Och, it's just so you're no' standing out in the cold like," Julian said. "They'll probably no' be out their scratchers for hours."

"They're actually awake, they're just not here," she said.

"You know I love a gossip, 'mon in," he pulled his head in, fussed with the chain, then opened the door for her.

***

"You lot are always running about," Julian said mostly to himself, as he messed about getting the kettle on the little gas hob. "No time to just sit and smell the roses."

"Iona and Roman are in a lot of trouble. Arabella, even more," Holly said, and like a fire hose it all came tumbling out of her. All of the stuff about her memories, Nicnevin, the Seelie Court. "I don't know what to do."

"Well, sit down first," Julian said. "You look like you're about to pass out!"

She sat down, and Julian looked at the kettle. "Maybe coffee is a bad idea."

"No, I need the caffeine," she said. "That would be great. I've probably been up for twenty-four hours at this point."

Julian grumbled. "That's not good for you, you know."

"If I don't act fast, the others are done for. I'll sleep when I'm dead."

Julian scratched his goatee. "I don't know about all this Seelie Court business, but you're all pretty powerful witches. There must be some way to get back. How did you get there the first time?"

"It took most of a day. And even if I could get back there, I don't know where they are *now*. No, what I need is to contact them."

"Well, that shouldna be too hard. You lot are always on your phones these days."

"My phone doesn't work. And even if it did, I don't think they get signal there." She thought back — those weird dial tones she got when she tried phoning Arabella.

Julian, looking acutely aware of his inability to offer constructive help, went to fetch a tray of biscuits.

"They could be dead already," she said. Her mind was going a hundred miles an hour. "They could be dead and I'm just sitting here."

"No use thinking the worst," Julian said. "Keep calm, let's work out a solution. You're a powerful witch, I've seen less powerful witches do incredible things with less."

Suddenly she remembered Nicnevin's face, dripping blood. Her words.

Holly gasped in her seat, flinching at the mere memory.

"No, I'm not," she said, quietly. "My power is a sham. It always was."

Julian's brow knit. "I don't know about that."

"Nicnevin, she said drawing magic from this city was a sham. An illusion. And she was right, I could *feel* it. I can feel it now." She twisted her fingers through the air, pulling ribbons of green light from the weave of magic. But she could see under the verdant tones, a sickliness. "I didn't see the horrors under it. Or worse, I could, and I didn't want to."

"Your magic is like Arabella's?" Julian asked. His image was flickering between the faun and the glamour. "Glasgow magic?"

"Yeah..." Holly said. "And now I'm not even sure I should be using it. Roman and Iona looked at me really weirdly when she said that."

"Roman and who?" Julian said.

Holly raised an eyebrow. "Iona."

Julian looked at her blankly. He lifted the tray of biscuits for her.

She pushed it away gently. "Julian, I need you to tell me you know who Iona is."

Julian looked vaguely confused, as though she'd asked him a

question and he'd immediately been distracted by something else.

Oh God. Whatever it was, was starting.

"I need to talk to Arabella. As soon as possible," Holly gulped. Before she apparently forgot who they all were. "We spoke before, in the Underground. But I couldn't open that circle again, not by myself."

"Well, when Arabella needed a bit of oomph for a spell..." Julian thought. "She always went to the crossroads."

Holly looked up at him. "Oh, my God."

Arabella standing on the crossroads of Union Street, Jamaica Street and Argyle Street. When she'd cast the Glasgow Curse on that guy. She'd said!

Julian blinked. "Did I spark a thought?"

Holly jumped up out of her chair. "I completely forgot! How did I forget that!"

Julian sipped his tea. "Did I help?"

"You might just have!" she said. "Thank you thank you thank you!" she shouted, putting her coffee cup down. "I've gotta go, I should do it before anyone wakes up!"

"Godspeed, wee witch," Julian smirked, taking a hobnob as the bell on the door jingled and she ran out the front door.

***

Holly walked down the road as fast as she could without breaking into a sprint. While she did it, she recited everything she could think of about the others. She tried to fix the image of them vividly in her mind. The little details. The way Roman's bleached hair curled, the smell of Iona's perfume. The way Arabella had smiled when they'd first seen each other again.

She arrived, doubled over, gasping for breath. The crossroads was pitch-black, just as it had been on the night they'd been walking home with the cyclist.

"When the Apocalypse finally comes, the portal to hell will open right there. Like a fault line in an earthquake."

Now that she was paying attention, now that she was sober and actually thinking magically...

Of *course* she could feel it.

She sat down outside the Waterstones book shop, closed her eyes, and concentrated.

Breathe in.

Breathe out.

Breathe in.

Breathe out.

With each breath, she became aware of her lungs filling and emptying. The weight of her legs on the cold stone of the pavement. The connection, directly to the ground underneath her, like a fish floating on the surface of the ocean.

The air was pretty clean, this early in the morning. The car fumes had had the entire night to clear. The ground under her was still, the echoes of the rumbling trains at Central Station not yet starting to wake.

She reached out, with her mind's eye, into the ground beneath her, trying to tap that energy she could feel. But even now, she could sense the dark undercurrent in it, the twisting tentacles in the deep. It made her pull her hand back, reflexively, as she would from an open flame.

She tried to skirt around it. If she could just pluck the bits that didn't make her feel that way, she could gather enough strength to get a message through to Arabella.

There was a moment as her lungs filled with air, when her perception seemed to flip — like one of those pictures where it looks like a person, but then suddenly like two people in conversation. A dress which was blue and is now gold. The air flowing in was the solid now, the atmosphere around her a living beast. She was not an individual, but a receptacle, empty until the air filled her. The entire Earth one being, one organism. Alive.

The World Tree. It was here, through the rift. She could grasp it with her hands, feel the bark of it.

"Arabella?" she asked.

The tree grown from the cyclist shivered as the message passed through it on its way through the cosmic branches.

"Arabella?" she asked again.

There was... not a silence. Closer to a static. The low hum of the universe, background radiation. She could feel the dark energies starting to encroach as she continued to use their magic.

"Come on Arabella..."

"Holly?" a voice came back. It sounded like she was somewhere with a lot of people talking in the background.

"Arabella! I'm at the crossroads! I'm here to help!"

"I'm in triage."

"Triage?"

"It's like a trial," Arabella was talking under her breath.

"How can I get to you? What do you need?"

"Honestly? I need my friend here..." Arabella said. *"You managed to find me all the way out here — can you pull yourself through?"*

"I... maybe. Here, Arabella, I think Nicnevin might be right. Glasgow magic is... dirty. It's full of evil. Should we even be claiming it?"

"Lord and Lady, Holly, I never had you down as a Puritan."

Holly canted her head, her brow furrowed.

"How did you manage to get so deep into Glasgow magic without noticing the nonsense of thinking we're completely perfect?" There was a tinge of annoyance in her voice. *"Do you honestly think I was claiming joy in being Glaswegian while not noticing that we're living in a hive of people that want me dead? Multiple things can be true at once, Holly! You don't fix the wrongs in the world by ignoring them, you bring them to the surface. You address them. And when you have privilege, you use it to change the*

rules of the game on behalf of the people who are hurting."

Holly coughed. "Well damn."

"Now are you coming to help me or not?!"

"Yep! Coming! Coming!" Holly said. Her stomach still lurched when she turned her mind's eye downwards towards the mass of Glasgow energy below her. The deep inky unending sea carried by the Clyde.

She grabbed it with both hands and gripped it tight.

"You fucking listen to me," she said out loud. "You're going to obey *me* now. You're gonna take me to Arabella, or I'm gonna rip you out of the ground like a fuckin' weed."

It spiralled up her fingers, entwining her, trying to pull her in, make her one with it.

And it was then, as the panic response started to kick in — she got it.

She had to be, *unbendable.*

They lived in a world full of bigotry, of corruption, of selfishness. The governments wouldn't help. The police wouldn't help. All they had was each other.

But they were far from powerless.

With Iona and Roman, with Arabella, this force could not break her. And in return, she could stop it advancing, she could hold it back. She could *force* it back.

She twisted it, and felt a gap open up between the branches. The world shimmered.

chapter 28

Holly sucked in a breath as the world moved.

She was sitting down in a pew. A hand grabbed hers. It was familiar, and comfortable.

"Arabella," she said, turning to her friend.

"Thanks for coming, pal." She wrapped her in a hug. It was clearly an attempt to hide that she'd been crying, but it didn't work. Holly squeezed extra tight.

It was only then she realised that she could hear Roman's voice in the background.

She looked around, taking in the surroundings. A large, luxurious rustic room with wooden pews in which they all faced the door. Behind them, she turned her head slightly and saw Roman orating to Nicnevin and a group of people who were all as large as her, in various shapes.

"He's doing better than Iona did," Arabella said.

"I was talking to Julian back at the shop, he couldn't remember who she was!"

"They wiped her memory off the world," Arabella said. "Everyone will start to forget her now." She was welling up again.

"How do we stop that?" There was a steely resolve in Holly now that wasn't going to just get brushed away.

"We need to turn the other two judges against Nicnevin. This whole thing hinges on the idea that Munro and I are..." She looked at Munro, standing behind Nicnevin's chair like a bodyguard, eyes glazed over, shoulders slumped.

Roman was in top form, playing conversational table-tennis with all of them at once.

"She's my property," Nicnevin said. "At the end of the day, your friend is a thief."

"Eh, don't shit in my cauldron and call it a love potion, hen," Roman said. "Cos where I'm fae, you don't *own* other people."

"She owes me a life-debt. Her life is *mine*," Nicnevin said.

Roman rolled his eyes. "Ugh! You sound like my mother. How many *lives* must she pay you, Nicnevin? Even if by some legal loophole her life belongs to you, *clearly* her heart belongs to another. Even a witch of your calibre can't change someone's heart. Not in any way that counts."

Arabella muttered to Holly. "He's got them bickering. That's good, people never want to stop an argument in mid-flow."

"What does she mean, she owes Nicnevin a life-debt? Why does bringing her back mean she belongs to her?"

"It's not exactly..." Arabella said, but she trailed off. Holly looked, as Arabella tried to force a word out, and she concentrated.

There was a golden magical thread that had sewn Arabella's mouth shut. She could just barely make it out, but it fizzed like Irn-Bru when she tried to talk.

"What the hell?"

Arabella groaned. "I'm not allowed to talk about it."

"Nicnevin again?"

"Yeah. It was a condition of the deal. I can't tell you," she said. She thought about it, then looked away. "But… it's like, *right there*. It's in this building. I could *show* you."

"What?"

"Can you remember how to astral project? I showed you before…"

"Maybe a little?"

"Hold my hand, I'll walk you through it," Arabella grasped her hands tight. Her nails were digging into Holly's hand a bit, but she didn't say anything. They started to synchronise their breathing, Holly looking all around the room.

"Honestly, I don't really get the nature thing," Roman was saying. "Sorry to say. I was born in concrete, and I'll die in concrete. I'm a city rat, through and through."

The woman with the horns snorted into her hand, smirking like Roman was an amusing court jester. Nicnevin was clearly trying very hard not to show that it was bothering her that he was doing well. But a look round the room, and she spotted Holly in the pew with Arabella.

She blinked, in shock. Holly clenched like she'd just walked out into the road without looking.

Nicnevin turned back to Roman, but she looked like her mind was racing.

"She can't single me out while this is going on," Holly said. Then she laughed. Oh my God, a bit of good luck for once. "It would make her look bad that her spell failed, or I one-upped her."

"Ready?" Arabella said, redoubling her grip on Holly's hand.

"As I'll ever be," Holly said.

They closed their eyes, and opened their third eyes.

"Eye of newt and bark of elm,
Let us travel in the astral realm."

***

Holly felt everything start to spin away, when a hand squeezed hers. "Ready to go?" Arabella said.

She could feel the pew under her bum still, but also, they were standing in the aisle. "Lead the way."

They ran towards the door, and Holly made an instinctive move to push it open for them, but then they passed right through it. They were out in the corridor.

People bustled past, all seemingly working, but none of them noticed Arabella and Holly speeding past them, Arabella quietly keeping count under her breath.

"It's around here somewhere, I..." she said, turning her head this way and that.

"Can we ask for directions?" Holly said.

"Well, no-one can see us unless they cast a spell to," Arabella said. "And I'm pretty sure anyone we asked would just haul us back to the courtroom. Let me remember, it's just been a while. I think it's in Section D?"

"Wait, how many times have you been in here?" Holly said.

"A lot," Arabella said. "When..." she trailed off as her teeth seemed to magically cement together when she tried to finish the sentence. She groaned and gave up. "Just, follow me."

Led by the hand through the bowels of the municipal building, Holly was starting to worry she wouldn't be able to find her way back to her body. As she thought about it, the thought seemed to burgeon in her brain like a weed, anxiety building as she started to become aware that she had no sensation other than still sitting in the pew.

She took a deep breath and centred herself.

Arabella turned and looked at Holly, up and down. Reading her aura. She squeezed her hand tighter. "Your magic's gotten so strong."

"People keep saying that to me," Holly said. "I don't understand what they mean."

"It's as if when Nicnevin wiped your memory, all the theory of magic left your head, but you still had the muscle memory. Your mind remained open. That's why the memories kept sticking, no matter how many times they were covered up. You are... this fountain of untapped potential. An explosion of unrestrained possibility."

"Alright, give it a rest. I'm just a person."

"No..." Bella canted her head. "I can't even see the limit of your power. But I am excited to see where you go after this." She grinned.

Holly cringed under the painful sensation of being observed.

Arabella stopped at a door marked *'Library'*. "Here's the ticket."

"You pulled me out of the courtroom to check out some books?"

"No, clever clogs, it's oral history," Arabella said, passing through the door and pulling Holly along behind her.

The room was definitely not a library. It looked more like an apothecary. All along the walls, large bookcase shelves floor to ceiling, each one packed with jars of varying sizes and shapes. Inside each jar were fireflies, or glowing amber liquid.

It smelled like a library though. The dry smell of old books, being taken off the shelves and leafed through. The thick smell of biro ink from people taking notes.

"What am I looking at here?" Holly said, but as she spoke, she felt a voice like a power drill in the back of her head. She clutched her ear.

"Ms. Morrow. Are we not keeping your attention?" It was Nicnevin.

"Oh shit," Arabella said, and she vanished like a wisp of smoke.

"Arabella?" Holly looked around. "Arabella!"

The image reappeared, flickering like the signal was bad. "She's called me up. They pronounced Roman guilty. I ha—" And she disappeared again.

Holly looked around the empty library. Now what?

***

She took a few tentative steps through the library, surrounded on all sides by the glowing amber lights of the fireflies in jars. She padded through the aisles, looking for something, anything, that Arabella might have wanted her to see.

Holly tried to lift a few of the paper tags tied round the neck of the jars, but her hand passed right through. A few of them she could read though as the tag faced outwards.

'Cillian IX'

'Christmas 1974'

'Griselda going to Lochwinnoch'

So, what, they were like magical VHS tapes? What was the purpose of them?

When she came to the end of the aisle, she came out on a reading nook, with an assortment of artefacts on plinths. A woman facing away from her was polishing what looked like a clay dildo.

"Beautiful, isn't it?" she said.

Holly jumped.

"Yes, I'm talking to you," she said, turning to face her, looking her right in the eye.

"You... can see me?"

"I'm a librarian, I see everything." She had a very silky voice, long hair in braids of many different colours, Indian skin tone and narrow shoulders over which a blue Prince Charlie jacket and kilt were draped. Holly felt a strange aura coming off her, like there was something familiar about her.

"Do I know you from somewhere?"

The librarian smiled. "Yes, you do."

"Sorry, I've been having trouble with my memories recently, I don't remember meeting you."

"Oh, we haven't met in person," she said.

"I'm lost," Holly said.

"I know you are," she said. She lifted the clay dildo. "Isn't this gorgeous?"

"Cock is not really my thing," Holly said.

"This dildo belonged to 17th Century Scottish lesbian Maud Galt. She was accused of witchcraft."

Holly arched an eyebrow. "I see."

"Very little documentation of historical lesbians in Scotland," the librarian said. "This is an antique."

"Yeah, even when *I* was growing up it was like 'you're going to be lonely forever, it's a sad existence'. Except then you grow up and you're happy and comfortable and you find your place, and the only sadness in your life is the people who didn't accept you." She watched as the librarian put the clay piece back in the cabinet. "Wait! I forgot!"

"What?"

"I came here to find something. My friend, Arabella. She's on trial right now, and she says that if I know the circumstances, I can turn the other judges against Nicnevin."

"That sounds pretty intense," the librarian said. "What was her name again? I'll look her up." She walked back to her desk and started leafing through a large book.

"Arabella Morrow."

As they were talking, a group of fireflies flew down from the ceiling and into an empty jar by the large tome.

The librarian groaned. "Ugh! Two in one day?" She pulled a cap and screwed it tight so they couldn't escape. She put a hand over the jar lid and took a deep breath, then wrote a name down on the tag: *'Roman Buchanan'*. "This one's got a cool name," she noted.

"That's my friend!" Holly shouted. "Roman's my friend, what is that?"

"This is where he goes when everyone forgets him."

"I haven't forgotten him though!"

"You will." She made sure the cap was screwed on tight. "Memory's a fragile thing."

"What is this place?"

"It's where stories go when no-one passes them on. Everything ends up in here, catalogued away. Eventually."

"Arabella said it was a library!"

"It is," she said. "Biggest library there is. Aha!" she said, pointing it out. "Arabella Morrow. Doesn't look like anything's been manually removed from her head though. All we have is residual."

"It won't be from her head — she still remembers it all, she's just not allowed to tell me."

"Then who am I looking for?"

"Her girlfriend? Munro...? I don't know her surname."

The librarian raised an eyebrow. "Munro Selkiefolk." Her expression darkened. "Sorry, that's confidential."

Holly groaned. "Her life's in danger! Please!"

"I'm under strict orders from the Seelie Court not to let anyone access the memories of Munro Selkiefolk. She belongs to Nicnevin, and therefore Nicnevin's privacy extends to her."

"What the fuck does that even mean!" Holly shouted. "Everyone keeps saying that, that Munro *belongs* to Nicnevin. She's a living person, she's not someone's property! What the fuck kind of deal do they have going on?"

The librarian tensed. She was biting her lip, as though doing arithmetic in her head.

Holly took a step towards her, but the librarian put her hand up before Holly could reach her.

"I could blame it on England, I'm very good at that," the librarian said to herself pensively. "And it's not like they don't deserve it."

"What are you—?"

"If," the librarian said hesitantly, "Say someone had accidentally left the memory out." She looked it up in the book and started scribbling down a reference on a card. "And didn't see that you'd seen it..." She winked, loudly. She slid the piece of paper across the desk.

Holly made to pick it up, but her hand went right through the desk. The librarian slapped herself on the forehead, before flipping the card over.

It read, *"Shelf I2C43, Row 4."* She spent a few seconds committing it to memory, then looked up at her. "Thank you."

"I don't know what you mean," the librarian said, and started performatively whistling Skye Boat Song as she went back to what she was doing.

Holly nodded and started running off.

"Wrong way!" the librarian shouted, not looking up, and Holly turned and tore off in the other direction.

chapter 29

The jar she was looking for was bigger than the others. The contents rattled around inside like they were trying to escape. Holly could touch this one, like the fireflies had some astral weight.

"Before you do this," the librarian said, standing at the head of the aisle. "Are you absolutely sure you want this?"

"I don't have a choice."

"That's not what I asked."

Holly unscrewed the cap on the top of the jar in answer. As she felt it start to give, the glass seared hot suddenly, and smashed in her hands.

Glass and flame shattered outwards in a radial pattern, Holly gasping as the world seemed to slow down and —

The library was gone.

In its place, a shimmering world of radar and background radiation. A stony beach, the people and the rocks and the ocean rendered in glittering sapphires and diamonds. It was not unlike the recreation Iona and Roman had done in Arabella's bedroom oh so long ago.

"Where am I?" she asked.

The reply of the librarian seemed distant, bodyless. "These are Munro's memories. They've been locked in here, to stop her talking about them."

Sure enough, there was Munro climbing onto the shore, dragging the carcass of a dolphin behind her. Blood dripped from her mouth and smeared down the front of her selkie coat.

"How long ago was this?" she asked.

She could hear the librarian start to reply, but it was smothered by the wind and then she was gone, as she felt herself ground in the dream.

Holly approached, softly — as though Munro could see her. She watched as Munro expertly stripped the skin of its flesh, throwing it in a rope net she had been keeping around her shoulder. There was something almost clinical about it that made the gore even more unsettling, as she reached into the chest cavity and ripped out the heart, biting into it like a juicy red apple.

"You're quite skilled at that, aren't you?" The hair on Holly's neck stood on end as Nicnevin spoke from behind her. She turned. The resplendent form of the Witch Queen of Elf-hame, lying on the beach as though she were sunbathing in the light of the overcast day. With her teal skin and her size, she almost looked like a large pond, or a rivulet left behind by the tide going out.

"Who are you?" Munro said, on edge. "This one's mine."

"Oh, I've no interest in your catch," Nicnevin said. "I just like looking at you."

Munro looked puzzled but went back to what she was doing when she'd confirmed that Nicnevin wasn't going to step in on her space.

"What's your name?" Nicnevin asked.

Munro finished eating the last ventricle, wiping the dripping juices from her lower lip with the back of her hand. "Munro."

Nicnevin smiled a wicked smile. "I'm Nicnevin."

A shot of fear took Munro's face. "Of House Nicnevin?"

"Oh aye." The smile didn't fade. "You've heard of me."

"Everyone's heard of you, Your Highness. Often right before they die. Are you going to kill me?" Munro said. "Only I'd like to know if I should bother running."

Nicnevin rolled over onto her front, looked at Munro like a toy in a window. "Maybe." She rested her chin on her hands, removed the sunglasses she'd been wearing from her face. "Will you be here tomorrow?"

"I'm here every day."

"Maybe I'll be here too," she said.

Munro lifted the carcass over her shoulder. "I can't tell you what to do."

Nicnevin watched her leave, unmoving.

***

Holly watched as they met, day after day. Weeks turning to months.

"My lady," Munro said, swimming up onto the beach and shedding her skin into human form. "I've brought you something."

"Oh, have you now?" Nicnevin was in the same place as always, lying across the rocks like a beckoning siren. "I do like when you bring me things, dear."

Munro put a small token at Nicnevin's feet. It was made of shiny rock and bits of broken glass she'd recovered from the beach, tied together with twine. A black feather stuck out of the back. She'd spent a lot of time on it.

Nicnevin picked it up, not unlike if her cat had brought her a mouse. "Aw, thank you dear." She paused as long as she could before saying, "What is it?"

"A charm," Munro said. "Selkies don't have much magic, but we do know how to make those. It will keep you safe."

"I love it," she said. She reached forward, rested a hand on Munro's cheek, and kissed her deeply.

Holly touched her mouth, feeling the memory of Nicnevin's gentle lips, her tongue, of Munro's heart quickening to a hummingbird's in her chest. She felt a guilt settle in her stomach, spying on such a personal memory.

She spun her hand, fast-forwarding the memory when she understood the way the story was going.

***

They were fighting back-to-back in some kind of war, Holly sped through. Nicnevin unleashing mighty spells on waves of enemies, Munro cleaving the skulls of anyone who got close to her.

She started to feel the candlewick of the dream burn out as she was fast approaching the end.

Munro, wizened and old and short of breath, lying bedridden.

An old smile creased her face as Nicnevin entered. "Hello, my love."

Nicnevin looked the same as always, but her face was streaked with tears. "Hello."

"Have you come to say goodbye?"

"No," Nicnevin said. "No, I haven't." She reached her hands out, and Munro took them.

"You've stretched my life this far, Nicnevin. I fear I may snap if you try and stretch it further. I'm ready to go."

"No," Nicnevin said sharply, wiping the tears from her eyes. "No, Munro, you're not. You're ready when I say you are. I am your Queen, am I not?"

Munro smiled. She could barely keep her eyes open. "I don't have the energy to argue right now. I'm ready to rest." She patted her hands. "We aren't meant to live forever, your Highness. Not like you..."

Her eyes closed.

"Munro... don't leave me," Nicnevin said.

Munro didn't respond.

"Munro?"

The memory was fracturing around Holly now, as Munro's brain started to stop.

Nicnevin's voice started to fade. "No... Munro, stop... no..." But the darkness was filling the room, until the only light was her. She began to grow brighter, and brighter, and brighter, until Holly had to cover her face with her hands, a burning star and the room started to fill in—

Munro gasped in the bed, taking in ragged air and coughing as her lungs fought collapse.

She lifted her hands, watching the passage of time reverse, as inevitably as the tide going out. "What happened, I—" She rested her back against the headboard. "I don't feel good."

Nicnevin was crying. "You're alive! I did it, I brought you back!"

"Nicnevin, why do I feel like this?"

"You'll get used to it, it's just my soul pinning yours to your body! It'll be fine!"

Munro put a hand on her chest, feeling her heart beat normally. "I don't like this," she said. "I was ready to go. It was my time to leave."

"And now you don't have to!" Nicnevin said. "Oh, I'm going to have the cooks make something special tonight. How marvellous! I can't believe I didn't think of that sooner! Well. Necessity is the mother of invention I suppose." Nicnevin kissed her on the forehead and rushed off.

Munro was left on the bed, alone, still feeling her heart beating in her chest, and trying to process this.

***

Holly started to fast-forward again. It had felt like the memory had been about to burn out but now there was all this extra time at the end. Munro following Nicnevin about, this weight in her stomach. Holly could feel it, and then—

A flicker of happiness. A strong one.

She stopped the feed.

Munro on a beach, just out of the Glasgow Outwith.

"Hello."

It was Arabella. Tucking her hair behind her ears, collecting shells in a basket.

"Hi," Munro said.

"This is where we come in," Holly said out loud.

The memories moved quicker now, fuelled by young love. But they were hurting Holly's head now, because she was in some of them. It was all starting to thicken and come together like a soup.

The ceilidh where Holly had first met Munro that Hogmanay.

Holly sitting on the couch, flicking through a magazine, with Arabella rushing about her all a-flutter.

"What's got your pants in a twist?" *she said out loud, echoing the memory.*

"I think we're, I think." Arabella stopped, clutching a dress in her hands. "I think tonight's the night!" She was vibrating with excitement.

Holly whooped like a hyena. "Yes!"

Arabella beamed, fighting back a blush.

Holly howled like a wolf at the full moon as Arabella ran in hyperactive circles around the couch.

Holly — the real, current Holly — laughed, remembering it. Why had she had to forget this? Why had Nicnevin been so selfish that—

The memory came to Nicnevin in their same living room. Looking down on them from the skirting of the high ceilings that were so bloody hard to heat.

"Okay then. Wipe my memory," Holly had said, clenching her fists.

"You're a witch, a witch's memories are not so easily tampered."

"Then take the whole year," Holly said, chin jutted out in defiance.

Her whole life had been this. A posture, chest out, chin out, eyes wide. A snarl in the face of a bully. "I've only known witches even existed for a year. You could wipe every trace of magic out my head with a snap of your fingers. And spare them."

"Holly no, I can't let you do that!" Arabella said. Munro was holding her back. "You'll lose everything you worked for!"

"If the choices are, Nicnevin murders you, or this, I choose this. What — I lose you, or I lose my magic? Not even a decision."

Arabella was scrambling at Munro's hands to let her go.

"Arabella, I choose you. You're my best friend in this whole world."

Nicnevin rolled her eyes. "Touching. Well. I suppose if everyone has their memory wiped, I'll say no more about it."

"You can't wipe my memory, your Highness," Munro said, darkly. "Any more than you can wipe your own."

"Yes, well," Nicnevin said. She sucked on her bottom lip, quaking, though she spoke in clipped tones. "Maybe you'll learn not to do this again, Ms. Selkiefolk."

Arabella drooped, and Munro let her go. She ran to Holly. "I'm sorry Holly, I'll do my best to keep you safe. I'll try and keep the magic in your life."

The two of them hugged, as Nicnevin waved a hand over the two of them, and the memories began to slip out of their ears like fireflies in the night sky.

***

The dream collided with the present as it caught up, leaving Holly gasping for breath back in the library.

The librarian was looking around as all the fireflies started to dissipate. "Oh dear, Holly Winter. You are in very big trouble."

And then, her astral form was pulled back into her body in the courtroom.

Stunned silence.

Holly looked at Arabella in the stand, then at Munro, still mind-controlled behind Nicnevin. All three of them mortified.

"I'm sorry," she said, voice cracking. She watched the fireflies dancing around them and realised that everyone in the entire building must have just seen what she'd seen.

"How... *dare*... you," Nicnevin said, her skin now chalk-white. She started to loom over the entire courtroom, the lights dimming to a candle flicker as her eyes began to burn like coals in her skull.

Holly stepped back, out of instinct, as Nicnevin raised her hand, a swirling maelstrom of purple energy flowing around it, and brought it down on her.

chapter 30

Holly flinched, closing her eyes as the purple force barrelled towards her like Death on his pale horse.

But it never reached her.

She opened one eye, then the other.

Out of the fireflies, standing before her, were Arabella, Iona and Roman. Hands raised, in defiance of the spell.

"How did you—?"

Nicnevin snarled. "I'm going to have words with that damned librarian. But I can send you all back as quickly as—"

"Well hang on a moment, Nicnevin," the other judge with the butterflies on his face said. "I don't think you're being entirely fair."

"Fair?" Nicnevin said. "*Fair?* They stole from me—!"

"That's what you've been telling us, but the memories say differently. Did you bring *her* back to life against her will?" he nodded to

Munro, who was staring at the floor, completely unaware of what was going on.

"I did think it was a bit strange," the other judge said, scratching her billy goat beard uncomfortably. "I didn't want to say anything, but why do you have her puppetted? I thought you two were in love."

"Yes, Nicnevin, we overlooked this strange mortal fetish of yours when we thought the two of you were in love but…"

"She's mine! My love! My heart!" Nicnevin said.

"She is her own!" Arabella shouted, stepping forward. "She didn't want to be here, but you forced her to be, and now she can't even live the life you gave her!"

"I'm sorry to say it Nicnevin, but I think the mortal's right," the fairy lady said. She rattled her fingers in the air, revealing golden strings suspended above Munro. They creaked, and then snapped, dropping Munro to the floor.

"Hey, you can't do that!" Nicnevin said, as Munro gasped for breath on the floor.

"I can do whatever I want," the fairy lady said. "If you have a problem with it, our houses can go back to war."

"You would threaten war for the life of a mortal you don't know?"

"I would threaten war because you're doing my nut in, you old hag!"

"How fucking dare you!"

"Ladies, ladies," the butterfly man said, pacifyingly.

"Don't you fuckin' start!" the fairy lady looked past Nicnevin and pointed a finger at him. "Condescending wee prick."

"Yeah, who the fuck do you think you are?" Nicnevin said.

On the floor, Munro gasped for breath. She looked up and started to sneak along the side.

Iona turned to Holly. "You continue to impress me, young lady."

"We're not out of here yet," Holly said. "Though, oh my God it's good to see you." The four of them had a big hug.

"The party's all here!" Roman grinned. "The four of us together, Nicnevin better watch her back."

"The five of us," Arabella said, unable to contain her joy. She turned, and Munro collided with her in a hug that enveloped her and lifted her up off the ground. She laughed.

Holly smiled. Even at this dark moment, it warmed her heart to see it. To see two people so in love.

They kissed like they'd been drowning.

Munro put a hand on Arabella's face. "Hello, my beautiful witch."

Arabella smiled. "Hello, you old sea lion."

"— and another thing, you cantankerous old—!" the butterfly man was shouting, but Nicnevin had stopped. She was staring at Munro and Arabella. "Nicnevin? The least you could do is pay attention when I'm shouting at you!"

Nicnevin's lip was quivering like a wean's. Her eyes were going puffy and red.

"Nicnevin?" the fairy lady said.

"It's not fair," Nicnevin whispered. "It's not fair. That was us. That was *us*."

The butterfly man tutted and took Nicnevin's hand. "Och you daft cow." The two of them gave her a hug, and she started to bawl.

The spectators had started to file out, as though worried they were going to get in trouble for watching this sad turn of events.

Holly put her hand on Arabella and Munro's shoulders. "Go to her."

"What good will that do?" Arabella said, under her breath.

"*Go to her,*" she insisted again. "We still need to get her to leave us alone. Maybe now you can convince her."

"Or it could get my head chopped off," Arabella said. But she looked around at her coven, at Munro. "But hey. I think she'll find it pretty difficult to wrestle me into a guillotine with you lot around." She took Munro's hand, and they approached the Witch Queen.

***

"Nicnevin?" Munro said, approaching. The two of them were shaking.

Iona and Roman took Holly's hand, chanting under their breath a ward of good luck, for all the good it would do.

"Oh, what do you want now?" Nicnevin said. Her throat sounded raw, huge globuling tears still running down her cheeks, but she didn't seem to have the energy to wail anymore. "Come to rub it in? Your happiness?"

"No, I came to see if you were okay, your Highness," Munro said. Her eyes were red too. "I still care about you."

Nicnevin scoffed. "You have a funny way of showing it." She looked to the ceiling, wiping under her eyelid to catch the tears.

"I could say the same to you," Munro said. "Tying me in strings like Pinocchio?" She gave a little chuckle. "You daft old hag."

"Oh, come now, is that any way to talk to your queen?" She started to pat down her skirts as though trying to reclaim some dignity of sitting on the floor.

"I will always care for you," Munro said. "Some of those times were the happiest of my life."

"Then why can't it stay that way?"

"Because things have transpired between us that..." Munro said, and she stopped. She made a groaning noise. "You know I hate talking about feelings stuff, why are you making me say it?"

"Because I don't understand! Why don't you love me anymore?"

"I fell in love with you. And I gave you my life, and you gave me yours in return. And when I was ready to move on, you pulled me back. And... this second life feels... empty. I feel like I'm hanging on by my back teeth, like every time I close my eyes I might slip away. I feel like a walking corpse. But every time I told you this, you waved it off. You ignored what I was telling you. You didn't care."

"The alternative was death!"

"It was my time! I told you that much! I lived to be 400 years old, all my grandchildren, my great-grandchildren were dead! We had several lifetimes, and I loved you, but... I was done."

Nicnevin rubbed her eyes. "Then what does *she* give you?" she nodded at Arabella, who curled away. "If your new life is so meaningless, why do you need to spend it with her?"

Munro looked at her and her eyes positively glittered. God, Holly thought — she needed to find a woman that would look at her like *that*.

Munro sighed. "She makes me feel brand new. Like it's not a second life at all, but a new one."

Arabella clutched the pendant around her neck. "Munro..."

Nicnevin stopped. "Okay..." she said, barely audible. "I get it. You're right." She took a deep breath, like she was letting go. "I'm sorry."

Munro smiled. "Thank you, my Queen."

"Oh, I'm not *your* Queen anymore," Nicnevin said. "She is." There was still a slight hint of bitterness in it.

Arabella scratched the back of her neck awkwardly. "Oh, I don't know about that, ma'am..."

Holly snorted.

Munro laughed, then rubbed her chest. Like she was suddenly having trouble breathing.

"Munro?" Arabella said, as Munro's grip on her hand began to go slack. "What's wrong?"

"I don't know, I..." she was breathing deliberately now. "I can't... get air..."

Arabella looked at Nicnevin. "What did you do? What did you do to her? Nicnevin, what have you done?"

"I... nothing, I—" Nicnevin said, worried. Then, realisation dawned. "Oh no…"

Munro keeled over backwards and hit the ground hard, gasping and heaving.

Holly and the others rushed up, Iona running a hand over her to reveal glowing pathways of orange through her.

"What's wrong with her?" Holly said. "What's happening?"

"The necromancy that brought her back," Nicnevin said, sadly. "It was my spite that kept her here. When I renounce that…"

"Nicnevin, that's not— she *just* got this new life!"

Nicnevin cringed. "I'm sorry. There's nothing I can do."

Arabella rushed to Munro's side, cupping her face. "Munro, Munro look at me."

"I don't want to go," Munro said. "Not now, not after all this. I don't—"

"Shh, save your breath. It's not over yet!" she looked to Nicnevin, rage cutting through the fear. "You are going to help her. You're going to help her, now."

"I can't!" Nicnevin said. "There's nothing I can do! I bound her soul to mine to keep it here! As soon as we parted ways…"

"Bullshit!" Arabella said. "You're the strongest witch in Elf-hame, there must be *something* you can do!"

"There isn't," Holly said, interrupting. She swallowed. "But like you said Arabella. Witches are stronger together."

Arabella turned to her. "What are you talking about?"

"When Nicnevin was going to send me to hell, you all banded together and tweaked the spell. Changed it slightly, sent me home. Could we do that here?"

"Tweak it how?"

"If her time's up, if the universe is calling her to return to the earth, maybe we…" Holly shrugged. "Make it so the universe doesn't notice for a while?"

"What, we *trick* entropy?"

"It's just a rounding error, people make them all the time," Holly said. "Iona?"

Iona shrugged. "It... could work. Maybe?" She looked at Nicnevin. "The entire coven, with the help of three Very Powerful Arch-Fey?" she said pointedly.

Nicnevin nodded. "Of course."

Roman put his hands on Holly and Arabella's shoulders and squeezed. "Come on, folks. Let's save a very hot and burly woman's life."

***

The four witches of the Coven of Merchant City stood around the heaving body of Munro, calling the four corners.

Above them, towering, the heads of three Houses of Elf-hame.

Holly had never felt so invincible in her life.

"What is life but a little time?" she called, as the others echoed.

"A blink in the eye of the sublime!

We witches call thee, near and far!

Bring your strength to heal this scar!"

Smoke began to coil around them, power forming, Munro at the eye of the storm, gasping for breath. Arabella stepped into the center and held Munro's neck up. "I've got you, love."

"Skip a spoke in the cosmic wheel!

A spare moment for this woman seal!

Slip a thread in the cosmic stitch!

A small fortune for a deserving witch!"

Arabella and Munro kissed, as they repeated their spell, golden light weaving around them like smoke, like twine, like a patch knitting over the world.

Holly felt her skin start to burn as the magic in the circle caught fire, burned like a star pushing back the void.

Holly could feel it. The moment the spell would need to take hold, to patch over the laws of nature. She reached deep into her well, and—

The void looked back at her. The darkness beneath the light.

Her skin crawled. She was drawing on it, using it. She pulled back—

A hand on her shoulder stopped her.

She looked back, away from the light, and saw the librarian.

"The good. And the bad. You have to own it all," she said. "Remember."

And suddenly, Holly knew who the librarian was.

The light consumed her now, and she couldn't see anything as the magic bent the laws of physics over its knee and snapped them like a twig, and they entered a place beyond time.

She could hear Arabella's voice in the wind — another memory from long ago? One of those impromptu witchcraft lessons on the carpet in the living room.

"There are as many ways to be magical as there are ways to be queer, or female, or dark-skinned, or disabled, or fat. Just by existing you have broken the determinism of the universe, all of society's programming telling you what to be. You are. Despite what they want you to be. That is the strongest magic in the world. Why do you think those with structural power co-opt our language? Terrified, they appropriate our strength. But they can't. Because to them, we are mistakes. We complicate their narrative. But we're not mistakes, none of us. If we were truly mistakes, they would've been able to erase us by now."

When the light faded, and they could see, Arabella and Munro lay entwined in the centre of the scorched magic ring. Munro was breathing normally.

chapter 31

"By the goddess..." Arabella said, breathing a sigh of relief and pressing her forehead against Munro's.

"You saved me," Munro said, grinning. "I can't believe it."

"How do you feel?"

Munro blinked. "Fine. Good. Amazing?" She put a hand on her own chest, feeling her heartbeat.

"How much time did we buy her?" Arabella said, looking up at Holly, at Iona, at Nicnevin.

"Could be an hour. Could be a month. Could be ten years. We have no way of knowing."

"In fairness, that's kind of how life works anyway," Holly said. "You could be hit by a bus tomorrow."

"Oh, I'm not complaining," Arabella said. "Thank you."

Holly turned around. "Wait, where's the librarian? She was right here."

"I swear, if I could fire that librarian," Nicnevin said.

"She helped me, in the spell," Holly said. She was still a little dizzy. "I have to go see her. I'll be one second."

She ran off, before anyone could object.

***

The librarian was back in the library, sweeping up the glass of the shattered jar.

"I know who you are now," Holly said.

The librarian looked up and smiled. "Wasn't a secret!"

Holly tapped her temple. "You can hear what's going on in here."

"Well, you are a part of me."

Because Holly could hear it now. When the librarian spoke, it was at once the harsh nasality of Glasgow, rising into the rolling music of the Islands, the powerful weight of Doric - like the brisk sea wind was pushing it into the back of the throat. And then it fell into the clipped pan-loaf of Morningside and Kelvinside and all the affectation in between. She was Fyfe and Galloway, Inverness and Orkney - a diaspora stretching from Northumbria to Norway. She spoke English, Scots, Doric and Gàidhlig. She had been Pictish and Celtic and Irish and now, she was Pakistani and Italian, Turkish and Chinese and everything in between. She was Catholic, Protestant, Presbyterian, and she was Jewish, and Muslim, Buddhist and atheist, Sikh and Hindu and Pagan. She was the hopes and dreams and patriotism of 5 million people collapsed, like a superposition, into one. The living, spoken memory of the land which was now known as Caledonia. Alba. Scotland.

And Holly could feel the pride radiating off of her in waves. *Come home*, it said. *Everyone*, it said, *can be home here.*

"Even the English?" she asked, out loud.

The librarian shrugged. "If they behave themselves."

Holly laughed. "Sorry for smashing your jar."

"Och I'm sure there's more where that came from." She tipped the contents of her dustpan into the bin. "I'm glad your pal's okay. I do like the odd opportunity to fuck with the Seelie Court."

"What you said in the courtroom," Holly said. "When you said... I have to own it all."

"Well. Your forefathers would very much like to forget their sins, but that seems somewhat unfair to their victims."

"Arabella said the same thing. But she seems to be able to still feel proud of where she's from despite there being so much wrong with it."

"Well, are you gonna fix it?"

"I'd like to," Holly said. "Very much so."

"Well. That can be a kind of patriotism. People don't love the *land*. They love an image of the land, usually one that paints them in a good light. When it makes pretty postcards. When it makes them noble."

Nicnevin's words in Arabella's cell sat in her stomach like a rock.

"It's like you! You only had part of the story. Even now, with those memories back, you don't *remember* anything from before you were born. And how much do you remember after that? Of your own life? Ten percent? Five percent? But you can't live a life cataloguing everything from every conceivable angle — even if you wanted to, you only have one perspective. So, you make it up! You make up your own life! You decide who you are, and then as you interact with the world, you change! You become different! And then, you make up all this other stuff on top of the stuff you already made up! Make up money. Make up ghosts. Make up gender. You know, human beings are remarkable. They create *worth*, just by existing. When there's no observable truth, they make one."

"Okay, now you're collapsing into 'is anything real' and I have to stop before my brains come out my ears," Holly said. "I can't abide that shit."

"I only mention it because that's the heart of your problem. What truths are unobservable because they were... hidden? Sometimes maliciously, sometimes by accident, sometimes out of shame. Each human being is an irreplaceable, unique miracle, creating the story of one life, retelling the story every time you remember it, a little differently every time." She was looking at Holly now in a way that made her feel uncomfortably like an ant. "And there are seven billion of you all bouncing off each other! Passing things on, choosing what is real and what isn't. An unbroken orchestra that's been playing for 64 million years, and right now there are seven billion voices in it. And you feel this... clash. This cringe. When you meet someone who hasn't been singing in your bit of the choir. Like say... when you meet some white American claiming Scottish ancestry through a relative they don't even know?" she finished, pointedly.

Holly rolled her eyes. "It still bothers me... There was something about it, like — you don't know the first thing about us. And you don't really care."

"No, you're right, he doesn't. But in his story, Scotland is some far-off, mystical land. It's out of focus, it's historical. But no amount of reading Wikipedia will change that for him. He would need to live here to see what you see."

"But doesn't it feel a little... fascist? Like they wanna claim these ancient Celtic heritages? Like they wiped their canvas white and then got bored and went looking for some flavour."

"But, on some level, Holly Winter... is that not also what Scotland's own do? This sterilisation process where we paint ourselves as good. As just. When we harken back to better, bygone days, ignoring the sins of our past? Or when we pretend a complex, structural problem is just the cause of a few bad eggs?"

"So, what, the alternative is pessimism?" Holly said. "How do we fix the problems our governments refuse to address, to build safety for the vulnerable, to right the wrongs we've committed? What's the alternative?"

She shrugged. "You tell me, hen. But I know it doesn't lie in ancestry. In blood. Blood will curdle on the ground, evaporate into the air. It won't stay. And it has no power to do anything but stain." She shrugged. "You all have voices. Some people's voices have microphones. But a crowd can always shout over a microphone."

Holly sighed.

The librarian raised an eyebrow. "Did you know... There's no such thing as a Scottish citizen?"

"Yeah, no, you're a British citizen living in Scotland. It's pretty shit. Like, no wonder there's all this weird angst about what it means to be Scottish when legally you're no different from a Londoner staying in an AirBnB for a weekend."

The librarian smiled. "Well. Call me a glass half full gal, but I always thought there was a silver lining."

"Oh?"

"If you live here, if you make your home here, your family, your livelihood, your *community* — you're Scottish. No appeal to heraldry. No claiming ancient bloodlines. Not a peep of 'oh my grandfather's wife's dog...' — it doesn't matter!"

"Hm. I suppose I didn't think of it like that," Holly said. "Who knows, maybe that line of reasoning would be encoded into a Scottish citizenship program if we end up as an... independent... country?" She grinned, poking the proverbial bear.

The librarian hung the dustpan and brush on the wall as though she hadn't heard her.

"Oh, come on — not even a 'no comment'? I gotta know what you think. You're probably the only person who could tell me how it's all going to play out! What's going to happen?"

"Holly, I'm not a fortune teller, I'm a librarian."

Before Holly could say anything else, the butterfly man burst into the room. "Yeah, so you all made my friend cry? And we helped you with your problem, so I feel like we're square now…"

"Uh, sure…" Holly said, a little taken aback.

"So… fuck off?" the butterfly man said. He waved his hand, and knocked the wind out of Holly, and then she was standing in the Archive.

***

She'd never seen so many people in this room. Roman was laying down a tablecloth, Iona messing about with biscuits and the kettle. Munro, still looking a bit peely-wally, was lying on the little couch by the door, holding Arabella's hand as she sat by her bedside.

It felt like home. Truly like home.

"Hi," she said out loud.

Roman looked up. "Oh, you're back!"

"Yep," Holly said. "Sorry I missed the first flight."

"Oh my god I thought that woman with the cow ears was going to backhand me across the mouth!" Roman said. "Let's maybe not cross them again?"

"Agreed," Arabella said. "Thanks everyone."

"We all clear now?" Holly said. "Can I sit down?"

Arabella smirked.

Iona put the teapot down on the table. "Put your feet up."

Holly sat down, and tried to burn this moment into her memory, so tightly no magic could wipe it away.

This was where she belonged.

epilogue

"It's weird to think this was where it all started," Holly said. The two of them were standing on that crossroads again, looking at the little tree sticking out of the building. It was now flowering, little pink blossoms.

"The rain's keeping it nice and fed," Arabella said, inspecting it. She looked at Holly. "I'm sorry this is where it starts for you. There's so much lost time."

"I remember most of it. It doesn't feel real, but I think I made the right decision all those months ago. It led us here, after all."

Arabella wrapped Holly in a hug. "You're a good friend."

"No, you."

"Ugh, stop!" Arabella laughed. "I hate when you do that."

There was a flickering by the tree, and they both turned to look, as Iona's astral form appeared. "Sorry to interrupt, bit of an emergency."

"What's going on?" Arabella said, stepping forward.

"There's a mermaid trapped in the Squinty Bridge. It's going to rip it apart. I've managed to turn prying eyes away but—"

"We're on our way," Holly said, turning and running. They made a beeline for the Clyde, and with a spell, lifted the river up to carry them along like kelpies on the surface, those two Glasgow witches.

"Oh my God!" Arabella shouted, as they came to the bridge, the seventy-foot tall mermaid trapped in the cabling. Munro was wrestling with its tail. "Munro, look out!"

"I'm fine, stop worryi—*hurk!*" she said, as the tail lurched and threw her into a building, leaving a huge crater.

"Never a dull moment, eh?" Iona said, hovering on her broom by them as she broadcast the spell to keep passersby away, and Roman used his magic to warp the cabling to try and free one arm.

Holly grinned. "Where'd be the fun in that?"

* * * * *

acknowledgements

Oh boy.

If you've stuck around this long, I'd like to say — thank you, from the bottom of my heart, for reading this story! The finished project looks nothing like what I'd originally planned, but I suppose that's always the way of things.

This book feels weird, as a project that I took from first draft to finished book during The Covid Times. The spectre of everything going on in the world definitely influenced the escapism of it, and most of the ideas which became the first draft were either directly or indirectly invented on our Little State-Mandated Walks.

The list of people I'd like to thank is too long to mention, but I can't pass up the opportunity to thank the following people, without whom you wouldn't be reading this:

To my wonderful writing group, who now more than ever were an incredible asset during the writing of this one. For getting me to sit at my keyboard for long stretches of time each week, for motivating each other despite everyone being locked inside, and for the incredible debates and conversations only real friends can have. Many of those conversations made their way into this book in one way or another. I love you all, and send you infinite Boudicca emojis.

To my structural and line editor, Shona Kinsella — who I think counts as this book's first proper fan? A fountain of positivity and professionalism, who found many places in the story where I had assumed everyone's brains made the same logical leaps I did.

To Maxie Mettler, for her wonderful, measured and incisive sensitivity readings — helping me to make Arabella a more realised, full character within these pages. If you seek her services, a small plug! She is available at fiverr.com/maxiemettler.

To my family, but in particular my mum. I like to think of all the things I've written, she'd like this one the most. It definitely has her fingerprints on it.

And finally, again, to you for reading! If this book moved you in one way or another, an Amazon or Goodreads review wouldn't go amiss and helps me immensely! You can check out my other books and future projects at lukebelcourt.com.

Thanks again,
Luke
4 October 2021

about the author

Luke Belcourt is a writer of LGBT adventure fantasy novels, born and raised in Glasgow, Scotland.

You can find info on future instalments of the Glasgow Witches at **lukebelcourt.com**, or on Bluesky @lukebelcourt.com – providing he still hasn't managed to escape social media and go live in the woods.

The Glasgow Witches will return in...

VAMPIRES IN PARK CIRCUS

Also by the author:

Vampires in Park Circus

Munro Selkiefolk is dying.

Four years ago, Arabella Morrow broke the spell which made her star-crossed love immortal, but miserable. They've been enjoying the time they have left. But now that the years are being measured in hours and minutes, everything is going wrong.

Munro's family are coming out of the woodwork, expecting their own resolution. Her ex is intent on pushing her way back in. And Munro herself seems to be pushing away.

It's on these most harrowing nights of Bella's life, a vampire comes to stay. A vampire who is trying to give up human blood, who was kicked out of her grandfather's cult.

But now that it's been brought to her attention, exactly what is going on in that mansion at the top of the hill?

And why is it bending the ley lines of the entire city?

Join the Coven of Merchant City as they enter their darkest chapter yet...